TODAY

TOMORROW

NEVER

SHERLINA IDID

Published by: Shariffah Norazlina Idid

Copyright © 2022 Shariffah Norazlina Idid
Illustrations by Books and Moods
Edited by Hooked on Words Editorial Services Ltd
UK Edition

ISBN: 9789672579519

*Thank you to my child for believing in my next
journey in my writing career.*

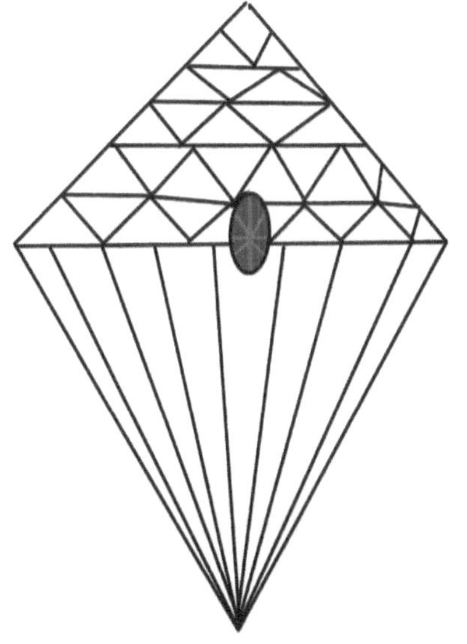

CHAPTER 1

The plane shakes left to right like dancing waves after hitting thick clouds that contain thunderbolts and electric charges from lightning. A naughty thunder electric spark wriggles and pushes itself into the thinning layer of fuel system. There is a malfunctioning of the plane-protected fibreglass and composite panels which spark a flame at the tip of the plane tail. Seats rock following the rhythm of the plane movements while lights flicker like a disco bulb.

'What's happening?' A passenger firmly grabs hold of an air steward's hand and shakes it as he passes by. The passenger's eye opens widely while his face turns pale.

'Sir, we are waiting for the captain's announcement. Please remain calm,' he replies.

Camelia's boots make a squeaking sound as she approaches her passenger seat after a toilet visit, and she feels the plane jolting up and down. This movement makes her feel jittery and slightly dizzy. Once she reaches her seat, fastening her seat belt, the feeling of losing a heartbeat roaming into her heart as the plane descending faster for a few minutes until it stops altogether. It makes her face turn pale. A few minutes later, it starts to descend further, this time faster than its normal speed. She feels her ears clogging with the drastic change in pressure. Then her heart pounds over a hundred beats per minute like a waveform from the patient heart machine. She grabs the handrail hard as the plane wobbles more aggressively. She wraps an arm around herself.

'This is the captain speaking. There is turbulence. All passengers, please remain seated and wear your seat belts.' Camelia and other passengers are able to hear the pilot's voice via the tannoy system.

From Camelia's spot, she noticed children cry loudly with tears rolling down their rosy cheeks; their hands and legs are flailing from side to side for help as their seats shudder. The turbulence leaves their mother in a state of shock, hugging their child for comfort.

Another passenger seated in the front row on the left of Camelia is turning his head left to right, his left leg shaking badly, his hands holding his head in his two hands and making his hair messy.

Suddenly, the cabin pressure reduces significantly. 'Argh. Oh my, I feel like I want to vomit,' she hears someone say.

'I can't breathe; I'm suffocating,' Camelia overheard someone else say.

Another passenger quickly loosens his tie and neck collar button, then breathes deeply to gather some air into his lungs.

Oxygen masks fall from the ceiling. Everyone is in haste to save their lives by placing the mask over themselves. Finally, a majority of the passengers' faces return to normal, and a new sense of calm settles in the air.

Camelia can't help but notice a lady reaching for her oxygen mask, the ceiling of the plane gives way. Beside her, a lady's head tumbles over her seat, as she isn't wearing a seat belt. Then her body which suffered a slight injury, was thrown in the sky at the broken ceiling.

Upon witnessing this, other passengers look in fear, sweat trickling down the side of every one of their faces.

They cling to their seats while tears roll down their cheeks and say, "I am too young to die."

Seeing the reaction from passengers, Camelia's hands tremble badly as she quickly places an oxygen mask on her face. Her complexion becomes pale. Within seconds, the plane shakes harder like a salt and pepper shake; she feels her whole body shaking and breathes deeply, places her head down on her lap. Hoping for protection in this position, her right hand firmly grabs the passenger's hand beside her for assurance.

She whispers a silent prayer ...

I need to survive for my mum's sake.

PRESENT

'Camelia! Camelia!' her mother's voice rings in her ears loud and clear as though she is beside her. She opens her eyes wide, staring at the cream-coloured ceiling. She shakes her head as relief washes over her. 'I am lucky; it is just a bad dream; I cannot imagine myself undergoing a tragic plane crash,' Camelia whispers to herself.

She goes straight to the bathroom to brush her teeth and bathe, preparing for the day's lectures. With the bad dream lingering in her mind, she murmurs, 'I hope today will be a good day at college.'

Camelia is a new student at Moonsriver college; she enrolled as a student two months ago, after moving to the town with her mother. Exactly two years ago, both lived in a town, Jacobsville, that is 296 miles away from the new town. Her mother was working as a freelance designer for advertisements. They shifted to the new town once her mother was offered a nine to five job at an advertising company. It was her mother's hometown.

Since she is in level eleven at high school, she often scores all A's in her science subjects. She was the top student in her previous college for Information Systems & Technology courses. When she transferred to Moonsriver college, a majority of the lectures and assessments she attended, she answered many of their questions accurately and quickly became the lecturer's favourite.

She never knew she would face difficulties being a top

student in this college. However, a few weeks back, after obtaining an A for an on-the-spot quiz, her fellow students began to feel intimidated by her presence. Especially, a particular five, who used to score ninety percent, primarily on quizzes and examinations; however, she beats them by getting one hundred percent.

Three weeks ago, after lectures ended, she noticed one from the five was busy graffitiing her locker with the words, 'Bitch lecturer sucker,' and, 'Show off bitch.'

Sometimes she finds creepy insects like fuzzy caterpillars and titan beetles falling off from her locker when she opens it. She doesn't like reptiles; therefore, they gave her the fright of her life. There is an occasion when a frog jumps out cheerfully from her desk into her oversized button-down top, jumping here and there on her chest. After this, she had to be placed in the sickbay because she struggled to breathe. The five students were laughing their heads off upon seeing her reaction. At almost every end of lectures, the same students would throw her nasty remarks to scare her off.

The countless bullying remarks, hiding fuzzy insects to scare her out of her skin, and mocking her in lectures by the five students make her feel unhappy. 'They should accept it as a means of a challenge for them to improve instead of making her feel afraid to attend her lectures. One day I should play a prank on them instead. Anyway, I am blessed to have Jen and Louise make my spirit high.' Camelia thinks to herself and smiles.

Camelia! Camelia! Stop daydreaming, hurry up, will you?' Mum's blaring voice is just ringing in her ears. The noise alerts her to brush off her thoughts quickly, and she pulls her long-sleeved shirt with 'No. 8' printed on it and grabs her school bag full of books before heading down the staircase.

Only to stop eye to eye with her mother.

"You're late! Come on, get in the car," Mum says, brushing her hair over her shoulder before adjusting her blue spectacles.

'Coming!' She skips a few steps from the veranda stairs, opens the car door, hastily sits down, and buckles herself in. 'I am here.' Camelia smiles at her mum.

In her early thirties, her mother adorns shoulder-length auburn hair with dimples that are visible every time she smiles.

'You will look neater if you tie your hair back, Cam.'

'I was in a hurry and totally forgot about it. I'll do it in a jiffy.

A few minutes later, their silver Toyota Camry parks in front of Moonsriver College's entrance. 'See you later, Mum!' she says and smiles at her mum before gently closing the door behind her.

Mum smiles at her in return.

She walks toward the college entrance as her mum pulls away, and she spots her two good friends who are waiting by the doors.

'Hi Jen, hi Louise! Come on, let's go in.'

'Hi hao zaoshang hao , Cam & Louise,' Jen replies.

'How was your three-day break? I bet it was lovely to see your sister from London?' Camelia asks.

'It was a busy day as my two nieces were a handful, but we went to the playground and amusement park while my sister spent time with my parents. Here is the picture of them, aren't they cute?' Jen asks.

'They are cute as well. They look like you, Jen,' Camelia replies. They inherit Jen's small flat nose with a square face with equally wide cheekbones with a touch of rosy cheeks. They tied their hair in a ponytail, looking adorable. Camelia wonders herself while smiling.

'Hiya! How are you doing?' Louise replies, smiling and waving at Camelia and Jen from the few steps away from the entrance.

'How was your break?' Jen and Camelia ask her.

'Nothing much, just helping around my dad's restaurant, trying to cook pasta but as usual it was a failure as I burnt the frying pan instead. Look at this scar on my hand,' Louise replies with a chuckle.

Camelia and Jen smile at Louise after hearing this.

'Jen, you do have a beautiful delicate 'cheongsam'.' Camelia cannot help but admire her friend's outfit, with its high cylindrical collar, side slits, and an asymmetrical opening in the front that stretches from the middle of the collar to the armpit and down the side. The opening is secured traditionally with knotted buttons top in royal blue, with a dragon embroidered into the material.

'We received a parcel from my mother and sister in Beijing, and I got this top,' Jen says with a smile.

Then the three eagerly enter the Technology building, making their way down the main hall for their lecture in Information Systems & Technology. Their lecturer, Professor Carlos, is a retired engineer for data scientists. He stands at the bottom of the lecture hall behind a podium, rubbing off the previous class notes on the board and shuffling through papers as the class settles into their seats.

'We'll be having a quiz today to gauge your understanding of my lectures for the past month. Please go to this link—' he points at the board where a short website link is written in blue marker— "and click submit once you have finished.'

It's summer time, so three sliding windows have been placed to one side so a nice breeze can filter in the lecture hall. The quiz starts within an hour, and the gust of wind with a cigar smoke plus a blue cheese odour comes from the window's direction. A majority of the students start covering their noses with their sleeves, and some cover with their scented tissues. Camelia quickly closes her nose by wearing an N94 mask that she keeps in her bag if required, which is handy this time. The smell is lessened with the mask on, and she smiles to herself because she was lucky enough to have brought the mask with her, so she continues answering the questions on the quiz.

The ten students sitting beside the three sliding windows are affected the most.

Once they have pushed aside their hair, thereafter they turn their heads and continue with the quiz by looking at the laptop placed on the table in front of them. After a few minutes pass for the quiz, all ten of them abruptly blink several times before suddenly opening their eyes wide. Camelia feels goosebumps covering her hands' skin when seeing their reaction. They looked in front and froze as though they have seen a ghost. Their faces turn pale, and their face muscles look stiff and sore as though they have been struck by lightning. Camelia's eyes blink when seeing their facial expression and skin color change. Then Camelia strained her eyes in the same direction as they were staring in front of a blank white wall, curious to find out for any items that caught their attention.

However, Camelia finds there is nothing peculiar; she shook her head. Sigh. Subsequently, she continues to finish the quiz. About ten minutes before the quiz ends. They move from their seats in haste, causing their chairs to fall on the floor in a simultaneous crash, pick up their bags hastily, then queue out of the door in a straight line. These loud noises and actions, has triggered Camelia to turn her head instantly; her heart started to beat faster; she accidentally dropped her auto mouse on the floor since her hand was shivering with the sudden change of event. The sound of her mouse crashing on the floor didn't distract those ten students. She picked it up while her head remained to concentrate on the face of those ten students, trying to figure out their actions and direction. Curious to know what they were going to do next, she got up halfway like a seated cum standing position to witness their successive movements. 'If I stand, it will obstruct those ten students, or they may just run after me. I better not stand.' At this moment, her heart is moving menacingly fast. 'I must see with my two eyes what are they going to do while starting such a commotion.' They march like soldiers from their seats toward the front of the lecture hall, then a man in front of the queue (the leader) opens the door widely, and they walk out. 'Why are they leaving so soon?' Camelia asked herself.

Camelia gasps. 'Look at their eyes!' It looks as though

they are under a spell. None of their pupils is noticeable. Their eyes are dull, and their gaze wander. Camelia appears worried for them with their bizarre behaviour.

'They look like robots. They are marching as though there is something or someone possesses them to walk,' Louise whispers.

Camelia starts to bite her fingernails while her right leg starts to tremble. 'There is something wrong with them. Could it be the odour they inhaled just now or the laptop radiation that caused them to act strangely? Camelia whispers to Jen and Louise.

'Someone should help them. I am sure they need help.' But, before she could raise her hands to suggest helping those ten students, the professor's voice interrupted her.

Professor Carlos shouts, 'All of you, return to your seats immediately!' while pointing his fingers at the group of ten students marching away.

At that moment, the lecture bell rings, and the students file out just as quickly.

CHAPTER 2

The lecture for today is over, thus Camelia is waiting for her mum to pick her up in front of the college.

'Bye Camelia, see you tomorrow,' Jen and Louise say as they walk past their friend, heading for their respective houses.

'See you tomorrow, you two.'

After an hour has passed, there's still no sign of her mother. Finally, she dials her mother's mobile, but it goes straight to the voicemail. Five minutes later, she calls her again, and this time the ringing stops, and she smiles since she's confident her mother will answer.

'Mum! Where are you?'

'Camelia?'

'You aren't my mother. Who are you?' Camelia asks.

'I'm Ben, your mother's colleague. I hope you still remember me. Please don't be surprised. I would like to inform you that unfortunately, I can't find your mother anywhere. Did she manage to contact you?'

'Hi Ben, I remember you. You are my mother's assistant that has been working with her team for a year? Mother introduced me to you during her office's family day last year.'

'Yes, you remember me exactly,' Ben exclaims in an enthusiastic tone.

'No. The last time I saw her was when she dropped me off in college this morning. I've been waiting for her for more than an hour.' Upon hearing Ben's statement, her voice changes cracks as she feels a rollercoaster of emotions seeping into her heart. She feels devastated and lost, with no idea how to locate her mother.

'Since all of my colleagues in my department have gone missing, can I pick you up from college, and we will file a report at the nearest police station?'

'Sure, that would be a good idea,' Camelia replies in a shaky voice.

'Wait, why are you helping me?

'You are my Project Manager's daughter, who is missing during office hours and my other colleagues. Therefore, there is a connection that your mum and my other colleagues have gone missing. Therefore, I suggest we both should report at the same time. What do you think?' Ben replied.

'That makes sense.' Camelia replies.

'I'll meet you at your college entrance. What is your location, please?' asks Ben.

'I am at Block A Sphere wing of the college entrance; I'll wait for you here,' she says. Camelia feels her heart beating fast; then, her leg starts trembling as she starts biting her fingernails.

A few minutes later, Ben appears before the college gates. She feels uneasy to be in the car with him, but her fear for her mother overwhelms her anxiety as she demands, 'What happened?'

He scrolls down the window screen and says, 'Get in the car, and I'll explain everything.' Once she opens the car door and takes her seat beside him, she notices his pants look dirty, smudged across the hem, and ripped at his left knee. His short dark brown hair is cut in a razor cut style in dark brown, and there is a heavy moustache on his upper lip. He looks sweaty and furrows his brow as he stares at her a few minutes without blinking. Is he dreaming or deep thinking?

'Excuse me, Ben, I feel uncomfortable with you staring at me,' Camelia says.

'I am sorry I didn't realize I was staring at you; I was deep in my thoughts because I am worried sick of my missing colleagues.' Ben replies.

While driving toward Casendra's house, Ben shares the story. 'Well, I believe it all happened after lunch, I noticed the timing when I got to the office. I arrived later than usual since I had the flu. I wasn't even supposed to be there at all with this cold.' Ben sniffles for emphasis before saying, 'The office was weirdly deserted, as though it was the weekend. When I got to your mother's work station, I found an untouched mug of coffee and her spectacles on her desk. But they're weirdly small. Look at this.' He fishes in the console before passing over the pair of blue-rimmed glasses that would fit a baby.

'In addition, I managed to download from security the CCTV that is placed at your mum's workstation, look she was alone in the office, the time is at nine in the morning as indicates in the monitor. She sits at her desk, switches on InDesign system that is in her computer, and poises her fingers over the keyboard; then, at the back of the monitor, smoke is released into the air. See… your mum tried to close her nose with her blouse sleeve. But it's too late as she inhales it. Instantly she stands up, marching away like a robot from her work table, then disappears as if into thin air.'

'How is this possible?' she murmurs. She shakes her head. Ben doesn't answer her question, but doesn't have much time to reply when her phone rings.

'Hello?' she answers her phone in a sad and cracking tone.

'Camelia!' Jen says. 'Are you at home? My family's disappeared.'

'What, Oh my God, I'm sorry, Jen. I'm not sure what's going on; my mother is missing, too,' she replies with a trembling voice.

'More bad news, Louise's family has disappeared too,' Jen replies, sobbing as Camelia is able to hear.

She feels uneasy with this additional bad news, suddenly unable to breathe, which causes chest pain. She has to bend down, holding her stomach as it's churning badly.

'Come and meet me at my house,' she replies to Jen in a faint, shaky voice.

'My closest friends' family have also disappeared,' she says to Ben.

'Yes, I overheard your conversation, sorry about that,' Ben

says. 'I guess my family have disappeared too as I couldn't get hold of my mother on the phone after calling her several times,' continues Ben.

'What could have happened to them, and who is behind this?' Ben says, the horror in his expression clearly making it hard to look Camelia in the eye as his gaze remains fixed on the floor.

His voice cracks as he continues to speak, 'I am really confused on what the possible solution is.' He continues to talk about his feelings on the incident.

Upon reaching Camelia's house, the car tires screech to a sudden halt.

'What in the world?' Ben exclaims.

Camelia's house is disappearing slowly from the left, inching to the middle where the entrance door is located. It only takes a few minutes before it evaporates completely like it had never been there at all. Camelia runs toward her house. 'My house! Why is this happening to me?' Camelia cries. She kneels and sobs on the plot of now empty green grass.

As she is crying and distraught by the disappearance of her house, Jen and Louise reach Camelia's house and run to her.

Jen and Louise shout at Camelia, 'Oh my god! Your house is disappearing just like how our parents and families have disappeared into thin air!'

Ben's hand is on her shoulder for reassurance. 'It will be okay,' he says. 'You're not alone.'

Curious about the change of events, Jen and Louise take the initiative to find out the incidents by walking towards

Camelia's neighbour on the right, facing the garden terrace. Both knock on the door but receive no response, so Jen peers through the window, looking for a sign that there are people in the house. But the light was still on in the living room.

Louise shouts, 'Anyone at home? We need help.'

Still, there is only silence. Her friends disappear around the side of her neighbour's house, and then after fifteen minutes or so, they return to where Camelia and Ben are standing.

'There is no one at your neighbour's house,' Jen says.

'What? None of them! Maybe they are having the same fate … missing.' Camelia starts sobbing, and her breathing is harder. 'Wait, let me call my neighbour. Maybe they are away.' Camelia sounds positive. But after several rings, no one answers her call. Her forehead is frowning with her mouth sprouting since there is no one. Her hands are fidgeting while holding and redialling her neighbour.

'Since there is no one in the neighbourhood to enquire on what is happening, why don't we drive to the city centre to check out whether it's all happening there too?' Ben suggests.

'Let's check it out first before going to the police station,' Camelia adds.

'Good idea,' Louise replies.

'Hop into my car now, ladies,' Ben says.

He drove a few minutes, then the car stopped momentarily at the traffic light; they spotted a TV in a shop window. Ben parks his car momentarily beside a pavement nearby the shop, and they stand before the window to find that the TV is showing a news channel. 'I am a reporter from TV Airthree.

A strange phenomenon has happened to our city. Reports have been shared with the police that people have gone missing after inhaling cigar smoke plus a blue cheese odour and looking at their computer screen. For the time being, preliminary incidents cause authority to make a decision that all citizen, "Do not open any applications! Repeat: never open any applications! People are strangely going missing after opening digital apps. Phones, computers, even gaming devices aren't safe to use at the moment. Only calling is safe at the moment.'

After hearing the news, unconsciously, Jen straight away holds her mobile, starts typing something. Camelia snatches it away.

'It's my phone! You have no right to take it from me!' Jen shouts at Camelia angrily.

'Don't you get it? Do you want to share the same fate as them?' asks Camelia.

Ben says, 'Using your phone for calling is okay. Thinking of it, it's logical since we only refer to the contacts section of the phone to call the person we wish to talk to; otherwise, don't even think about it.'

The car swerves as Ben tries to avoid hitting another vehicle.

'Ow!' Camelia shouts when her head hits the passenger dashboard of the car.

CHAPTER 3

'Wake up! Wake up!' someone shakes Camelia. When she opens her eyes, she's shocked to be staring up at the cream-colored ceiling of her bedroom. She blinks twice as her experience of witnessing her house vanishing, her mother disappearing, and the car accident was still fresh in her mind. Now, she is in her comfy bed. Camelia checks her hands, fingers, legs, and body; however, there are no bruises or cuts to signify that the accident occurred. Nevertheless, she is puzzled by the sudden change of events that she is currently safe at home.

She jumps out of bed and runs straight to the kitchen when she hears her mum singing. Her mum bustles around, preparing breakfast. This is weird, Camelia thinks. It was only just yesterday that her mum went missing and now she is happily preparing breakfast. What is happening? As she approaches her mum to hug her, a cat with fluffy white fur and ruby-red eyes sits on the dining table, meowing when it sees Camelia.

'Shoo! Shoo! Go away.'

Her mother's eyes widen with surprise and confusion. 'What are you doing? It took me a while to get Gummy to come into the house, and now you want him to go out?'

'What? Camelia pats hard on her mum's shoulder.

'Ouch! says her mother.

'Mum, since when do we have a house cat?' Camelia shrugs.

'Since last year. Camelia, don't you remember? I brought him home on the way back from work near Christmas, as he was shivering in the cold.'

Camelia frowns, perplexed.

'Oh! Look at the time, I'll be late for college if we don't go now,' Camelia says. When her mother only casts her a blank stare, Camelia insists, 'Mum, let's go!'

'Where are we going, Camelia?' Her mum frowns, and two of her right-hand fingers touch her chin to indicate she is thinking.

'To the college, of course.'

Mum is blinking in disbelief. 'Young lady, how many times have I told you that you need to walk? Why is today so special that I need to take you? I have lots of meetings to attend at work.' She glances at the clock on the wall. 'And I'm running late. I'm off.'

Camelia's mouth drops open. All her life, her mum has driven her.

'Mum.' Camelia touches her mum's left shoulder. 'But Mum, where were you yesterday? Ben was searching for you, and you forgot to pick me up from college.'

Her mother turns to face Camelia with lifeless eyes staring through her. 'I went to double-check something for the report. It took longer than expected. I forgot to inform you and Ben. As for you, I'm not supposed to pick you up from college at all. Was there any urgency for you to call me?'

This is unlike her. She picks me up everyday from college. She never fails to text me or call me to inform me of her being late and her whereabouts. What got into her? What happened to Mum? Camelia's mouth is dry as a bone, and there are butterflies in her stomach with the turn of events, and she doesn't know what to do.

All, except for one thing.

'I need to investigate,' Camelia murmurs.

***

At college, three of them, Jen, Louise, and Camelia, meet during break time since they don't have the same subjects for lectures today. Jen appears haggard with smeared make-up, unkept hair with her squeezing eyes shut, then opening them wide in an effort to stay awake. Louise looks anxious, with frowning lines visible on her forehead and mouth sprouting outwards. They pulled Camelia aside when they saw her walking toward her locker and walk further to hide beside Camelia's locker.

'Do you think there's something strange happening this

morning?' Jen asks.

'We were in the car with Ben yesterday evening, we got in an accident, and out of the blue, we're home, and our families are back and acting strangely,' Louise adds.

'You noticed that, too?' Camelia asks.

'Also, there are no cuts or bruises on any parts of my body due to the sudden minor accident,' Louise says.

'I second that, Louise,' Jen and Camelia reply.

'My missing house is back to normal, and my mum is back; her eyes have a whiter pupil, not her normal sapphire blue eyes, and she refuses to send nor pick me up from the college,' Camelia replies in an anguished tone.

It seems that those who went missing yesterday are back to their respective families, but why and for what? They are yet to find out.

'I don't want to risk using my phone for the news, but I managed to find my old Walkman. Let's see if they're saying anything,' Jen suggests.

'Everyone who went missing yesterday is strangely back in their homes. Local experts are puzzled with this phenomenon and are currently investigating further. However, all citizens are to remain calm and act as normal,' says the broadcaster.

'It will take a while if we were to wait for the authorities. Since the three of us have expertise in science and technology and award-winning Professor Carlos, we could discuss and plan to find out the solution. We should start the experiment first.' Camelia's voice cracks as she is about to cry.

***

Upon reaching their class, the ten students who robotically walked out of the lecture hall appeared normal the previous day, although their stares are strangely cold and their eyes have a slight ruby red glint like Gummy's. How strange, Camelia thinks.

Her eyes widen, and she momentarily stares at their eyes, then blinks in fear that the phenomenon might spread to her if she looks at them for too long. Her heart suddenly beats faster, and her shoulder hunches when she sits. Is there any correlation between the ten students, *Mum and Gummy? I am living with a stranger. Is Gummy a spy? Will I become like them if I touch Gummy? I touched Mum this morning, but fortunately, I haven't changed myself, so I guess I can act normal with mum. Why does whoever doing this want my mother, Jen, and Louise's family?*

'A star student is finally dreaming, lost in a space, huh?' One of the five students envious of her being a top student is here to mock her.

She casts him a glare.

'That is enough, Tim; stop mocking her,' the Professor interrupts.

Students need to go to the next class once the college bell shrieks for alerting students.

***

The next last class is the subject where three of them attend together once classes are over. 'Let's visit Professor Carlos in his office room, we need to discuss the strange phenomenon and how best we can find a solution. I hope his schedule is free, let's pay him a visit.' Upon reaching his office room, his timetable hangs on a small board beside the entrance. 'He is free at this moment.' As Camelia is about to turn his doorknob, she pauses when she hears some voices coming from the direction of his room. Camelia gestures at both of her friends to place their ears near the door to eavesdrop on the conversation with the ten students.

'All ten of you, please tell me what happened after you inhaled the smell from the window yesterday. By the way, I'm afraid I must inform you that you have all failed the test.'

One of the girls utters a word and begins speaking in a strange, robotic voice, too low for them to hear. As Jen tries to place her ear against the door, it flings open, and all ten of the students walk out of Processor Carlo's ten-square-foot room. Camelia and her friends scramble to hide behind the door.

Once the students round the corner out of sight, they quickly enter Professor Carlos's office room to ask him what happened to those students. But the room is empty. They search for him in the attached toilet, then turn their heads to face the cupboard full of books inside the office, just in case he's standing there. Next, they search through another cupboard full of books at the other side of his room for any clues of his whereabouts.

'There is a TV series I watched when I was a kid, with gadgets that zap a person. Hmm, let's check on the floor just in case they zapped him to a size of an ant,' Camelia suggests.

'You must be watching too many Marvel movies, Cam,' Jen replies while rolling her eyes.

Maybe he dozes off on the carpet hiding at the back of the enormous desk, and they are unable to see him from where they are standing, Camelia thinks. Louise ducks down and kneels beside the professor's mahogany desk. 'I can't see the Professor on the carpet,' she says.

Louise, who is the top student for chemical and biology subjects, takes out her magnifying glass from her bag and bends down to examine the carpet for any clues of his footprints. *She brings the magnifying glass in her backpack everyday since she likes to view plants and flowers.* 'He's not there. Where could he have gone?'

'I don't have a clue where else we can search for him, especially as we heard his voice in this office as well and didn't see him exit from this door,' Jen interrupts.

This is very strange. We cannot miss seeing him exiting his room. All three of us are standing near his office room door. We must have seen him if he were to pass by us. Is there a secret room for him to hide? Why should he hide? Hide from what? She shook her head to brush aside her thoughts.

CHAPTER 4

Feeling suspicious, the next day, Camelia came to college earlier than usual to check on Professor Carlos and discovers his room door unlocked. Once she enters his office room, her eyes open widely since she witnesses Professor Carlos looking blurry, as though he is about to fade into thin air.

As Camelia is about to speak, she hears him saying,

'It's time for me to leave for my lectures,' says Professor Carlos. He doesn't realize that his body size has reduced to a dwarf size. He must have changed his size after he shook hands with the leader of the ten students. This must-have happened during their private discussion yesterday. *I have a hunch that there is a chemical or electronic reaction between his hands with the team leader, which has turned the Professor a dwarf sized*, Camelia thinks.

Seeing Professor Carlos getting ready for lectures, Camelia quickly opens his office room door and walks off.

Her sweat trickles down her forehead, and she feels her heartbeat thumping faster than usual while walking toward her lecture class. She is lost in her thoughts, unable to believe that the Professor's body size has shrunk so much and he is fading. Can it happen after the ten students met him? Doesn't this relate to the odour and applications?

A few minutes later at the lecture hall, they stare at the entrance as the door opens by itself.

Then, walking toward the lecturer's desk, 'Look! Look! A flying book and a briefcase!

We cannot see Professor Carlos however, his book and briefcase are flying!' one student exclaims.

Some students discover the commotion, clearly afraid and puzzled, take their bags and run away, screaming, 'It's a ghost! A ghost! Help!'

'It could be our Professor Carlos,' Camelia whispers to Jen and Louise. *Amazing, a few minutes ago, he was blurry, and now he is invisible. Maybe he isn't aware at all that he is invisible.*

Let's assess our hunch by asking him a few questions. As they move forward, a few students exclaim, 'You three, you'd better be careful not to fall into the trap. If I were you, I would run away as far as possible.'

The student and his friends pick up their bags and walk away.

Three of them look at each other's eyes, then nod, agreeing to proceed with their suggestion to pursuit an answer to their hunch.

'Professor Carlos, is it you?'

'Yes, of course, can't all of you see me?' he replies.

But no one can hear nor see him.

His question remains unanswered. The books and briefcase he is carrying are shaking and turning, facing all three of them, and Camelia wonders if he is talking to them; however, they cannot hear his responses at all.

We can see the book he is holding is shaking slightly. He must be trembling upon seeing his students running panicked, saving their lives when they see him walking into the lecture hall without seeing his body.

He places his books that he was holding down on the lecture table, and the three ladies notice.

Camelia whispers to Jen and Louise, 'I will test his knee-jerk reaction toward pain in order to determine where exactly he is standing so we can guide him out to his office room for further questioning. What do you think of the suggestion?'

Jen and Louise nod in response.

Camelia smacks his shoulder to determine his reflexes.

'Ouch!' he exclaims. He is shocked by the pressure placed on his shoulder and instantly lets go of his briefcase, which falls to the floor.

'So in our experiment of the missing beloved Professor Carlos, he is actually invisible. Let me place a scarf on your neck so we don't miss you as we will lead you to your office room for our next experiment,' says Jen.

He responds by taking one of his books from the table and places it at the same level as his shoulder, then waving the book as an indicator to the three of them on his location. 'Thanks, Professor Carlos, we are now able to gauge the location you are standing in,' Camelia replies.

Three of them act natural while guiding the invisible Professor Carlos into his room. In order not to scare students around them, they walk in a triangle; Jen at the front, and Camelia and Louise on either side of Professor Carlos. With that, no one will ever notice the so-called flying scarf on the invisible Professor's neck. Upon reaching his office room, Jen quickly pushes the door open wide and takes Professor Carlos's invisible hands to lead him through the door so no one will suspect anything.

Closing the door behind them as they enter. 'Phew! We made it without anyone becoming suspicious of our activity. High five, girls!' Camelia says happily.

'Let me see, how can we undo an invisible Professor?' One of Louise's fingers is touching the tip of her forehead as she tries to think of a solution.

'We can't even hear his voice if he were to utter any words,' says Jen.

'I have an idea! I believe he can write down what he wants to say. Professor Carlos, please have a seat and write something on this paper,' says Camelia.

The three of them gasp almost in sync as they see the ink pen on the table moving from one side of a paper is placed on the desk to the centre, then its tip hits the paper, and a message is written there.

The three girls read the note together.

'Kids, when the ten students that were looking strange came into my office that day, ten of them hugged me tightly until I was out of breath. Then, there is a male, who I assume is the leader, who stared into my eyes as though he wanted to eat me alive or release a blue laser beam into my eyes. Next thing I knew, all ten of them walked away from my room.'

All three of them gasp, and Camelia's mouth opens widely at this new findings. She is confident there is a scientific and digitalisation justification on this. It cannot be magic or voodoo.

Suddenly, the sky turns to darkness, and it's night time. 'Oh my, look at the time, it is already six in the evening. We have been with the Professor for longer than expected.

'It's summer. Why is it so dark at this hour? Louise says. Camelia and Jen look at each other with eyes open in bewilderment. 'It is usually changes to darkness at this hour during summer when rain is about to drop from the sky. We better return home before rain falls; we do not wish to be drenched since neither one of us bring an umbrella,' Camelia replies.

There is a slamming sound, and then silence, and they're thrown into the blackness as the electricity powers off.

Louise's voice is dripping with panic as she says, 'Oh no, it's so dark. Erm, Camelia! Jen! Where are you? Are you still here?'

'We are here! You aren't alone,' says Camelia in a husky voice as she switches on her torch, but guilt drums through her when she spots Louise's pale face. 'Just joking, Louise.'

Louise grabs hold of an ultraviolet light small torch from her bag that she forgot to return to the college laboratory because she thought it was an ordinary torchlight. She switches it on, then feels more confident with the extra lighting. While walking toward Camelia, she accidentally points the light at

Professor Carlos's face.

'Oh my, what happened to your face?' Camelia sounds alarmed.

'What... what do you mean?' stammers the Professor.

'Your face...I can see it is half human and half... something else. I can't make out what it is. Don't worry, Professor Carlos, at least we know you're visible at night with the ultraviolet light from the torchlight,' Camelia says.

It's dark as the three of them walk home (leaving Professor Carlos behind in his room since he informed he has paperwork to complete), the street lights are flickering when they hear the footsteps of someone tailing them. They quicken their pace a little, clearly feeling the same tension. Jen starts biting her fingernails while there is a trickle of sweat dripping from Louise's forehead, and Camelia feels a sudden ache in her tummy as the sound of screeching tyres behind them grows louder. This is creepy. It sounds like heavy footsteps. Can it be a bear running wild at large? Will it eat us alive? I hope all of us will reach for safety soon, Camelia thinks. We are too young to die. Her palms start to feel sweaty with her fearful thoughts. They hear a branch break, and they spin around to discover two or three shadows are visible at the side of the bushes. They run as fast as they can toward Camelia's house as it's the nearest for the route they're taking.

Once the house is visible, they hold hands to help each other run faster. In a hurry to find her house key, Camelia accidentally drops it as she takes it out from the pocket and bends down to pick it up. Subsequently, all three of them scamper into the house, locking the door shut behind them.

They are all panting due to their fear of being pursued. Camelia draws her curtain slightly to the side to spot intruders around her house grounds. To her relief, she sees nothing but the dark evening sky above her neighbours' homes.

'The coast is clear,' says Camelia while switching on her entrance and living room lights.

They stay close together, still afraid of the unknown danger, when all of a sudden Gummy appears out of nowhere, which startles them all. Camelia and Louise were quick in their reaction, jump backwards for safety not wanting to annoy the cat. Leaving Jen standing at the same spot. Gummy sounds angry and scratches the bare skin of Jen's left hand.

'Ouch! You stupid cat!' Jen shouts with her eyes wide open, and her hand is about to slap Gummy, but she misses as the cat walks away quickly and vanishes out of sight. Camelia and Louise were surprised by Jen's reaction; their eyes open widely upon hearing this, their hands touching their neck while their mouth is slightly open.

'Mum, we are home!' Camelia says. The house seems quieter than usual as the lights dimmed, and the kitchen is pristinely clean like it hasn't been touched, which is strange. 'It's not like her to not be home like this.' As her friends cast her sympathetic glances, Camelia picks up her mobile and says, 'Hi, Mum, will you be late from work again? Can my friends stay overnight?

'I have deadlines to catch forgotten to inform you. Yes, you can spend time with your friends,' Mum says.

'Great…thanks,' Camelia replies.

***

Suddenly, watching from beside the sofa, they catch sight of a shadow moving outside the house. Their heartbeats are beating faster than usual, and as if in sync, Jen & Louise whisper simultaneously, 'I'm so scared.'

Camelia, the bravest of the three, heads straight to the window peeps through it but can't determine any intruder. After that, she switches on the garden terrace and entrance porch lights and sets the house alarm. 'Okay, now I feel much safer. I'm starving, so let's order pizza,' Camelia says.

'Hooray,' exclaims Louise, which Jen quickly agrees to with an enthusiastic nod..

While waiting for their pizza delivery to arrive, they enter Camelia's room, play guitar, and sing along to a song entitled *'Perfect'* by Ed Sheeran.

Jen, the introvert out of three of them, doesn't sing; Camelia notices that she was seating quietly on the bed with her fingers playing with her mobile phone.

The doorbell rings and Camelia's face lights up with excitement. 'Our pizzas have arrived,' she says.

Hurriedly, Louise and Camelia walk down the staircase, pass the hallway towards the entrance. Camelia peeped the side window to reconfirm that it is the pizza delivery guy instead of an intruder. As they open the door, Louise is standing beside the door holding a bat just in case she requires to safe Camelia, the pizza delivery guy from Dominos, is standing in front of the door. 'You ordered two large pepperoni pizzas, Ms. Camelia?'

'Yes, I did, this is the money, and thank you,' Camelia says after taking the pizza boxes. Upon closing the entrance door, a loud growling sound comes from upstairs, then it stops, but the girls shrug it off.

They tuck into their pizza, only to realize their friend is missing. 'Hey, where is Jen?' says Louise.

'We forgot to call her down,' Camelia says. 'Sigh.' She pushes her chair aside for her to get up, then walks a few steps upon reaching the foot of the staircase. 'Jen! Jen! Come down for dinner, princess!' Camelia shouts, laughing a little at the same time. But there's no response from Jen.

'Guess she must be in the toilet; she will eventually join us,' Louise says.

Suddenly, a growling sound resonates coming from upstairs and both shout, 'Jen! Jen, you lazy bum, come downstairs, dinner is ready!' They continue eating and laughing between bites, and the growling sound continues, coming from Camelia's room. Camelia drops a piece of her pizza on the plate while Louise stops munching her slice of pizza with her mouth wide open.

'I am scared; I can feel in my bones that the intruder is already in your house Cam.' Camelia nods, agreeing with Louise.

Camelia's heartbeat thumps in her chest as she realises her friend is right, and at the loud, deep growling sound, Camelia shoves her second finger over her mouth to indicate that Louise must be silent. She gestures at Louise to follow her upstairs quietly. Louise nods in agreement and pushes her chair carefully; however, the chair knocks against the wooden flooring, which causes a creaking sound to emerge. Louise freezes momentarily and gets up quickly as there's a space for her to do so without pushing the chair further and making additional noise.

Both walk a few steps away from the dining table located beside the kitchen, heading toward the foot of the staircase. Camelia looks steady, even though her shoulders are shrinking, and her eyes are open wide.

Both stop their movements momentarily. Camelia swerves to the side of the staircase where there's a long Chinese blue vase and where umbrellas and a long golf club are kept. She picks up the golf club, feeling braver with a weapon in her hands, then takes her first careful step. On the other hand, Louise manages to take the bat she was holding when the pizza delivery guy came. Fortunately for them, the middle of the staircase is covered with carpet, so it doesn't make any sound when they climb onto it. Upon reaching the second floor, Camelia extends her arms concurrently, slowly pushing her room door open inch by inch to reduce any cracking noises in the door's hinge.

Camelia's right foot enters her room inch by inch, moving forward slowly with her eyes and head-turning from left to centre then to the right of her bedroom. 'Coast is clear, nothing weird in this room except for a broken chair,' Camelia says to Louise.

Louise enters and goes straight to Camelia's window, as it was left ajar. 'Your room window wasn't opened just now?' Louise says as she peers through it. As she turns her head to the left overlooking the empty wall, she freezes momentarily as a 'were bear' look-alike in the dark appears. It's dark brown and furry, eight feet high, with a muscular furry tummy and paws as huge as a polar bear with sharp claws is looking eye to eye at her, it's eyes are in red bloodshot, looks furious as though he intends to eat us alive. He roared, looking at Camelia. Camelia was dumbfounded at this sound and the look on his face. Instantly he walks away from the spot, heading for the tip of the roof located just outside Camelia's window. 'Camelia!'

Louise, with her leg trembling, points her middle fingers at the creature, breathing heavily as sweat trickles down her neck.

'Wait! Who are you? What do you want from us, furry creature? 'Camelia shouts bravely.

Louise nudges Camelia's shoulder and asks, 'What are you doing? Do you want us both to be killed?'

Within seconds, it plunges off the roof as if to spread its legs open and jump, and both ladies notice the creature is wearing a pink ribbon with a Chinese dragon embroidery tied firmly at the back of its furry head, just like Jen's. The pink ribbon triggers them both to remember Jen, and they look at each other, frozen still and unsure of what to do. Wait.

'Where is Jen? Jen!' Camelia shouts.

They wear the same worried expression while searching for Jen in Camelia's room. Camelia pushes the toilet door open and switches the lights on; it looks undisturbed, and Camelia is relieved and can tell by her expression that Louise is, too. Louise walks straight to the bath tub, clearly feeling suspicious, extends her hands to draw aside the curtain open.

But there is nothing peculiar behind it, just a bathtub.

Once both are satisfied that Jen isn't in the toilet, Camelia closes the door behind her. As she turns her head, she notices that the lights on the ceiling of her wardrobe are blinking on and off. She stretches her neck and blinks twice when she notices her wardrobe door is slightly ajar.

Camelia and Louise glance at each other, then Camelia gestures at Louise that they should check out her wardrobe.

Louise nods in agreement. Both walk quietly across the bedroom towards the wardrobe built into the wall with two doors opening with mini shutters throughout its door.

Camelia places her hands gently on the material of her wardrobe door while Louise holds a golf club, ready to defend them from any potential intruders. A squeaking sound comes from the wardrobe's left side door as she opens it slightly, its automatic light continuing to flicker.

'Phew! No intruder here,' Louise says while wiping her sweaty forehead.

Camelia, feeling unsatisfactory with the findings, starts looking at the hangers with clothes for any intrusion, however, they appear untouched. 'Nope, she isn't here, either!' As Camelia closes her wardrobe door, Louise accidentally steps on something uneven and close to the wardrobe. She bends down and tears it from her shoe, frustrated that it's entangled itself around her heel. She observes and touches the texture as soft as the remnants of clothes that have been shredded into pieces.

'I wonder who they belong to,' Camelia says.

Both bend down and crawl toward the remnants that are

dark blue in colour, the pieces of fabric scattered on the floor near Camelia's study desk. Louise picks up all the pieces, adamant in finding the clue to Jen's sudden disappearance.

'Wait!' Louise cries, the sound stirring a new fear within Camelia. 'Jen wore a dark blue top today, right?'

Camelia stands to recall, and she replies, 'Yeah, you're right. Oh God, don't tell me it's Jen's,' Camelia says, her breathing quickening.

Louise starts to smell the fabric. 'It smells like the Guilty perfume from Gucci that Jen likes to spray,' Louise says, her voice trembling with fear.

'It can't be, I don't want to believe it's true,' Camelia answers. As they discover the last remains, they notice a pair of crumpled, faded blue pants folded underneath Camelia's study table. Camelia, who has the longest arm out of the two, reaches for the pants.

Louise peers around the room until she sees a thin brownish bamboo stick lying against a wall beside the wardrobe. 'The bamboo stick! Let me get it for you,' Louise says.

Camelia returns to her position by lying flat on her stomach, swaying the bamboo stick on top of the pants, puts pressure on the pants and pushes them, inch by inch, towards the desk opening. Once the pants are out from under the desk, Louise, who is ready to wear a pair of gloves, takes it from the floor. 'Oh my, these pants are covered with dust; you'd better sweep the back of them,' Louise says.

Camelia stands up and holds onto the pants; then her hands grab the side.

'What in the world!' Louise says.

'Oh! my, I just realized Jen was concentrating on her phone while we were singing, and she was bitten by Gummy earlier, could she be the furry creature that was at my window?' Camelia analyses loudly.

'On top of that, we found remnants of her attire; she may have transformed to the furry creature; how can we help revert her to a human?' Louise speaks between sobs.

As both become confident there is no intruder in the house; they climb down the staircase hurriedly with their noisy footsteps. Upon reaching the ground floor, the lights are non-stop flickering, and then within seconds, they blackout.

'Argh!' Louise screams.

'Where are you?' Camelia asks, trying to grab her mobile, which is located in the butt pocket of her pants and clicks on the torch icon on her phone. Unfortunately, her phone light shines directly at Louise's eyes, which forces her to close them. 'Oops, sorry, Louise,' Camelia says.

'Come on, let's go to the living room.' Camelia shines her torch from the left, centre, and right side, but Jen is nowhere to be seen. 'What is that? Shush... keep quiet,' Camelia says, 'I think there's something fishy in this house.'

Suddenly, a loud bang sounds, followed by a crash, as if a stone or something hard were tossed through the window near the house's back. Quickly, Camelia switches off her torch, and Louise manages to grab a small knife that's placed on the kitchen table, and both walk toward the guest room.

'911, we have an intruder at...' Louise blinks in disbelief.

At that moment, a shadow appears close to the broken

window. The curtain shakes ferociously as the cold wind seeps in.

I have a feeling the intruder or the monstrous creature is still lingering within my compound. Should I scream for help or should we overturn the intruder? Do we have the capacity with my Tae Kwan Do experience and Louise depending on the golf stick? What if the creature were to devour both of us alive, can anyone find our scarred bodies? Camelia thinks to herself.

'This looks scary,' Louise whispers.

Camelia brushes off her negative thoughts aside, breathing deeply to maintain her composure.

As they approach the guest room in the darkness with the dim light from the outside streetlights, a huge manlike shadow comes up behind them.

Seeing the shadow, 'I will be the heroine,' she whispers to herself and prepares her arms for a punch, even though deep inside she is terrified and longs to run away.

As they are about to turn their heads to see who the figure is, something pounces from behind them and sends them both into the blackness.

***

'Camelia! You are late for college!' Camelia's mum shouts.

'Erm…what? What?' Camelia opens her eyes, again seeing her familiar bedroom ceiling and trying to jump out of bed quickly. 'Ouch! As she turns her head to the right, she feels giddy, and a strange pain stirs in her tummy. She attempts to jump out of bed again and moves to the bathroom to get ready for college.

When she is in the toilet brushing her teeth, she notices that her usual shower curtain is drawn wide open, then she momentarily stands and recalls what happened the night before. After bathing, Camelia quickly skims through her wardrobe carpet for the torn clothes she believes could be Jen's, but there are none.

'Camelia! Why are you being so slow?' Mum shouts from downstairs.

'Wait a minute, Mum,' Camelia replies and quickly bends down to skim the surroundings of her carpet around her wardrobe and bed, however, there are no traces of Jen's torn top and jeans.

Her mother bangs on the door and quickly steps into her room. 'Girl, you are thirty minutes late for college! What are you doing crawling on the floor?' her mother shouts.

'I'm searching for my hair clip,' Camelia says.

'Go to college now; I won't have your lecturer complaining to me about your lack of attendance!'

Camelia scampers out of her room but momentarily walks toward the guest room to glance at the broken window, only to discover it's no longer broken. Curiosity overwhelms her, and as she reaches the window, her hands graze the centre of the glass to feel the texture. It's even; no sign of any damage can be seen.

Her mother appears beside her ear, which makes her jump. 'Mum, why are you standing so close to me?' she asks.

'Why are you so interested in this particular window?' her

mother asks.

'Don't worry, Mum,' Camelia says. As she turns her head, body towards the kitchen table to grab her breakfast, her mother is already standing beside her, her expression stern. 'Mum, you don't look well; I should bring you to the doctor.'

'No! No doctors, I'm fine. I'm just tired. Please go to your college now!'

Camelia manages to pop some cereal into her mouth before heading for the entrance. After munching, she pretends she has a stomach ache and cries out, 'Ouch! Ah, it must be the time of the month cramps; let me stay at home and skip today's lecture!' Camelia says.

But as she is about to run upstairs, her mother pulls her back down by the sleeve of her blouse. 'Wait a minute, girl, don't give me any excuses for being absent from lectures. I have paid so many fees monthly for you to attend the best college in town, 'her mother's tone becomes stern.

'But Mum,' Camelia tries to negotiate.

'You looked perfectly well a few minutes ago, so run along and meet your friends,' her mother says, finally persuading Camelia.

'Well, okay, Mum, if my stomach hurts more, I will call you to take me home.' Camelia kisses her mother's cheek.

Her eyes open widely as she is suddenly bewildered by her mum's skin texture, which is rough and slightly more uneven than usual. 'Mum, do you still apply moisturiser cream on your face?

'Yes, of course, why are you asking, dear?'

'Nothing, just asking.'

This is weird; Mum's skin used to be as smooth as silk; I wonder if her skin changed once she vanished or if Gummy is trying to turn her into…I better brush aside that thought. Wake up, Cam. She softly claps both cheeks to ensure she isn't dreaming.

Camelia closes her house door and walks faster than her usual speed as she realises she will be extremely late. But fortunately, after passing her friend Jen's house on the way to college, she checks her wristwatch and realises she's early; it's only eight in the morning. 'What a commotion, asking me to leave so early, huh?' Camelia mutters under her breath.

Camelia heads for Jen's house when someone grabs her left arms, just as Camelia is about to kick the person as an act of self-defence.

'Shh, quiet!' Louise whispers, pulls Camelia's blouse sleeves to one side, and asks, 'Do you still remember what happened last night?'

'The creature, Jen, suddenly went missing, the broken window at the back of your house then something hit us on our head. Did you get a bump on your head?' Louise asks Camelia.

Camelia starts touching her head, 'This explains the headache. Ouch.'

'I feel there's something my mum is hiding.' Camelia explains all the strange things she'd noticed about her mother that morning.'

'Why don't we sneak over to your house and check out what your mother is up to?' Louise suggests.

'Hmm, that is a good idea. Maybe she is planning

something with someone.'

'Quick!'

They head for Camelia's house, and while walking, they search for anything suspicious lurking outside her house.

Upon reaching the garden entrance, Louise pulls Camelia into a bush to stay hidden while also getting a better view. 'We mustn't let her see us,' Louise whispers.

Both walk slowly, careful not to make any noise. Both peep at the window located at the end of Camelia's house, overlooking the guest room. The room door bangs shut as her mother leaves the room, and both duck down under the windowsill as a shiver crawls up Camelia's spine.

Then Camelia rises to peer through the window but is now unable to see her mother anywhere in the house.

Suddenly, we both can hear the sound of screeching tyres against the tarmac nearby. Peering out of the window quickly, they watch her mother reverse her Toyota car and speed off. In the passenger seat is a man wearing an investigator-style hat in an ashy shade of brown, with white doctor overalls

Who is he? Camelia wonders to herself.

***

On their way to college, they notice Jen's house. They glance at each other with the same broad and fearful eyes. 'You know what I'm thinking?' Camelia says.

'Let's pay her a visit ! Maybe she is at home after all,' Louise says.

They turn to the left, planning to enter the compound of

Jen's house. It looks run down with its window blinds broken, the paint faded and deserted with long grass-grown on both sides of the lawn.

They walk cautiously, fearing the thought of snakes appearing. They hold hands while walking towards the entrance, gripping hard. Something about the house is uninviting, but Camelia can't work out what it is until she moves closer.

As they climb the three-tier high staircase located just before the entrance door, they notice a cat with a rusty orange colour with red ruby eyes watching them. It darts away when they reach the door. Camelia notices the bell and presses it, and listens to the ring. Then they wait for two minutes before pressing it again.

'Who is that?' a woman's deep voice shouts from within the house. Then the door swings open, and they find themselves staring at an old lady estimate age sixty with greyish bun hair wearing an apron, and Camelia and Louise smile in return at her. 'Oh, hello. May I help you?'

'Hi, Ms. Twistqy, it's us…Louise & Camelia. We are here to meet Jen.'

'How do you know my name, and who is Jen? Unfortunately, I don't have anyone by the name of Jen in this house.'

Camelia's eyes open wide in disbelief upon hearing those words.

'Ms. Twistqy, you have one daughter named Jennifer, and we have both been her best friends for fifteen years. Is she in her room?' Louise says.

'As I said, young girl, there is no such person in this house,' Ms. Twistqy replies, than slams the door in their faces.

This is weird; we just came here last week, persuading Ms. Twistqy to allow Jen to accompany us to Hawaii for a holiday. Ms. Twistqy was yet to give her decision, and now she forgets she has a daughter. Now I am worried. She must have forgotten her family.

Still feeling unsatisfied and adamant to find out what happened to Jen, Louise rings the bell. 'Apologise to disturb your morning Ms. Twistqy, but we are starving and thirsty. Our mothers left for work early this morning, so we are yet to have any breakfast.'

At first, Ms. Twistqy appears angry, as though she wants to scream at them; however, Louise's cute, pleading face makes her give in. 'Alright, you two, you may come in for water and some breakfast. You are lucky I was about to make pancakes, but you are to leave immediately, understand?' she says sternly.

They nod in agreement. When they enter the narrow old hallway of the house and walk toward the kitchen, Camelia notices a family photo hanging on the wooden wall beside the staircase. Louise, who is being nosy, pretends to miss her turn by going to the right, facing the foot of the staircase instead of turning left and heading for the kitchen. Camelia, noticing her friend's plans, holds Ms. Twistqy's hands and guides her into the kitchen. She shares her grandmother's recipes to distract the woman while Louise continues to walk ahead. Hearing Ms. Twistqy' s voice turns to delight while having a conversation on different types of pancake recipe with Camelia, Louise walks further. Once she reaches the family photos section, Louise takes out her mobile from her back pocket and starts to take photos of Jen and her family.

Camelia watches her subtly with little glances back and forth before returning her attention to Ms.Twistqy. Camelia starts to look at her wrist watch when the woman pours them the water. She quickly gets up from her seat and stands beside Ms. Twistqy, pretending she's learning how to whisk and place the pancake onto the frying pan.

'I need to use your washroom Ms. Twistqy,' Camelia says.

'Just turn to your left, walk through the hallway, then turn left.'.

'Right on.' Camelia slips away and follows Louise, knowing she doesn't have much time before Ms. Twistqy becomes suspicious, but the temptation is too much for her to refuse.

'What?' Louise mutters as Camelia appears behind her. 'You scared me, I thought it was the old woman. Phew! Look here…Why is this lady who resembles Jen named Beth? This is weird.' Curious to know who the person is, she turns her head to the side and spots a university book placed on an antique wooden table, located underneath the collection of photos. 'Maybe the answer lies within this university book.' Camelia whisper. Louise quickly turns the pages with Camelia looking over her shoulder. There are photos of the year 1967. As she flips the pages, she reads Beth Jennifer's name, Head of Cheer Leader's. As she closes the book, she retracts her steps.

'Urgh!' She turns to face the body she accidentally hit. 'What do you think you are doing, young girl, trespassing on private property, being nosy with people's personal lives! Leave now, or I will call the authorities!' Ms. Twistqy snaps, chasing both of them with her stick and closing the door in their faces.

'Let's go,' Louise nudges Camelia.

'One thing for sure, everything seems weird. Therefore, we must investigate and find a solution to this nightmare,' says Camelia.

Louise nods in agreement.

Camelia smiles to herself, thinking of a possible solution.

CHAPTER 5

Upon reaching their college, they hear a commotion, shrieking voices, and loud cluttering coming from the hallway between the students' lockers. They look at each other approaching inch by inch. At their spot, they see a crowd of students attentively peering at something alarming in the centre of the hallway, their faces creased in distress.

Camelia and Louise move closer to the scene; Camelia taps on a student's shoulder. 'What's happening?' she asks. The student turns, facing Camelia. 'Oh, it's you, Suzy from the Mathematics lecture.' Camelia smiles at her.

She returns with a smile. 'I heard Lucas accidentally took Henry's mobile by mistake. Henry accused Lucas of stealing his mobile to gather information against him.'

Camelia wonders who Lucas and Henry are. 'It's unwise for them to brutally fight over a mobile unless there is top secret information that Henry is very sensitive in sharing.

And they should settle amicably as an adult.'

'I reckon they are fighting due to Henry having a piece of sensitive information. I think it is more likely be a revenge situation.' Suzy interrupts. 'You are right; they should settle it like 'an adult.'

After a couple of steps, they shove themselves between the crowd to get a better look at the scene; they watch a fight unfold between Lucas and Henry. Lucas is a male student with broad shoulders, blonde crew-cut hair wearing a blueish greyish shirt, and Henry is one of the ten students affected by the odour from the open window at Professor Carlos's lecture.

From the spot she is standing, she can see Henry tighten his fist, subsequently, extend his muscular arms, and punch Lucas's face. Smack. The impact causes Lucas's head to tilt aside with visible bruises. Lucas's body is undeterred by the blow, still standing steadily. The collision led Lucas's face to turn red as an act of revenge, his hands fiercely clutches hard on Henry's bluish shirt, gripping it hard with his right hand, and his other hand casts him a blow. This impact causes Henry to breathe in and out rapidly while his jaw is dripping with sweat.

'It's mine. You have no right to it!' His voice sounds horrendous, like a shrieking wicked witch.

'He looks furious all over his face, clearly written on it. I hope both would not suffer any serious injury.' Camelia thoughts.

'Never!' Lucas replies. Henry's eyes are about to pop out from his socket, with his face looking like boiling with anger when he heard the negative reply. He ran closer to Lucas's spot, two of his hands squeezing Lucas's throat. He looks suffocated with no air to breathe; he then kicks Henry's tummy hard with him wearing thick leather boots. This movement leads Henry to release his grip and fall at the back.

'This must be awfully painful and tiring.' Camelia says to herself.

Huff and puff, Henry sighs loudly with his fist still clutching, 'You ain't getting any benefit with the mobile.' Henry wipes off his heavy sweat dripping the side of his sideburns. Then, starring face to face with Lucas. 'You need to be behind bars.' Lucas answers; after that, he gritted his teeth in anger.

That answer raises Henry's temperature; he cannot control his temper; he gives Lucas a blow on his jaw, then blood dripping like a drizzling rain at the side of Lucas's mouth.

'I think his lips slightly ripped off.' Camelia whispers to Louise.

Henry punches three times like a punching bag on Lucas's bulky chest without any remorse. Lucas shifts slightly from the blow. Then return to his position by blinking and maintaining his composure, wiping away the blood rolling down his mouth like a drizzle.

Both guys' breathing is heavy since we can hear the sound of their breathing. 'You'd better return my mobile in one piece instantly,' Henry shouts in his hoarse voice.

Lucas steps back a few steps, takes out an iPhone XR in blue, 'Look everyone, this is a photo of Henry with tons of drugs packets; he is a junkie. He sent this to the college WhatsApp group as a piece of evidence.' Lucas chuckles while his nose is bleeding.

'It is a setup!' Henry retorts.

Hearing this boils Henry's temperature, and many lines become visible on his face as his rage grows. Finally, he rapidly grabs hold of Lucas's shirt, carries him with his two hands in mid-air, and throws him on the floor.

Luckily Lucas's bulky body can withstand the throw, so he gets up and kicks Henry hard in his stomach. But he doesn't wobble and remains upright, and immediately grabs Lucas's leg, topples him, and lets go of him with a crash as his bulky body hits the ground.

Watching him breathing before Lucas can retaliate, he overturns Lucas by grabbing his waist. Lucas is struggling to hit Henry, and before he can do that, Henry throws him toward the steel students' lockers. Crash. Due to this incident, three students' lockers are poorly dented.

Lucas's mouth is severely bleeding, his shirt is slightly torn, and he's oozing with a black eye. Unfortunately, Lucas is suffering a back injury; he cannot get up.

'Stop!' Professor Edwin Lee, the Sports Disciplinary lecturer, appears and shouts. 'Everyone, go to your lecture hall now!'

The crowds disperse bit by Bit; however, Camelia and Louise are thunderstruck by the recent incident. 'What do you think? After mum acts weird, this scene includes Professor Carlos's invisibility, Jen's disappearance, and her mother's Dissociative Amnesia. So what the hell is going on?'Camelia whispers.

As they're about to leave the scene, they face the hallway

toward the lecture hall; ready to speed to the hallway, a gust of fast wind, consequently, leaves goosebumps to crawl up Camelia's spine.

Feeling suspicious, they turn their heads to face Lucas's body; from the location they are standing in, both are appalled to see a pool of blood coming from Lucas's body. 'We didn't notice any blood earlier…weird.' With their mouths open and breathing deeply, curious and feeling uneasy, they approach Lucas's body to determine that the blood is coming from his body. When they reach his body, both gasping in shock to look at Lucas's chest, Louise starts screaming her head off as they see his chest is ripped off with blood scattered around it. His torn shirt is drenched in blood, and his chest is bare. Camelia bends over, feeling a new tightness in her chest and churning her gut. She heaves and wretches on the ground. At the sight of her disgust, Louise begins to copy her. There are no organs remaining in his chest; his blood is seen dripping Bit by Bit from the location of his body, the hallway toward the entrance door.

How can this be? Who or what has taken his heart away? Camelia thinks.

Their legs and hands tremble. As they walk further front, they momentarily stop as they notice a few feet onwards, there are two tall figures standing like a statue. Upon reaching the two figures, their mouths drop open. Professor Edwin and Henry are standing, paralysed on the spot, as white as a ghost.

With her hands trembling, she dials into her phone, 'Hello, Ms. Lai., Help! Lucas's body is in the hallway, and I don't know what to do…' Then, in a panicked tone, she explains everything she saw, and only silence remains on the other end of the phone at first, until eventually, Ms. Lai answers quietly.

'I will get help. Please don't do anything.'

With her heartbeat pounding faster and breathing more deeply, Camelia says to Louise, 'We cannot ignore and leave the trace of blood without knowing where it ends, right? It may lead to the solution or answer to incidents that happened in our lives.'

Louise nods in agreement.

***

'Let's follow the trail of blood to determine where Lucas's heart was taken and who is behind this tragedy. I pity Lucas; not only he was hurt by the fight, but he also ended in a tragic death. But, it should not end that way,' Camelia says.

'If we were to wait for the police to arrive, it will be too late. The culprit is gone without any trace,' Louise adds.

Since they both feel pity for Lucas's injury and death, not trusting the authority to get the job done fast, they decide to follow the trail of blood, cautious not to step on murder scene evidence, and walk beside it, taking videos as they pass. Louise, as usual, the top student for chemical and biology, takes out her magnifying glasses from her bag. Determined to know whether there's any strange colouring to his blood, nevertheless, it looks normal, nothing weird. Then, as they're studying the trail of blood, they hear a sudden bang.

'The noise is coming from the entrance, ' Louise says.

Seeing the entrance door swing slightly, without thinking any further, they walk on the cemented floor cautiously toward the main entrance, following the trail of blood dripping starting from Lucas's body. Step by step, until it stops directly at an open entrance door.

She can hear her heavy breathing with sweat trickling down at the side of her hair. As they near the entrance as she's terrified at the thought of any monstrous creature that might be lurking as they open the door, grab and eat them alive. She brushes aside the tragic cogitation.

'Let's run toward it as you never know if the culprit is still lingering in the college compound hiding, trying to escape at the right moment,' Camelia says. 'At least we perhaps can witness the culprit for the police to catch it faster.' They run as fast as they can, panting while their heartbeat is beating faster than usual, eager to find the culprit yet terrified. Hopefully, we will get a good outcome, Camelia thinks.

As they arrive beside the entrance, they see themselves overlooking an empty pavement with a small, rounded fountain. A dripping trail of blood is visible at the centre. They skip the steps as they're trying their best to see a glance of the murderer or even catch them. The line of blood ends at one of the bushes nearing to the brick gate a few metres away from the college's main faculty entrance.

'This is tiring,' Louise says, panting.

Camelia freezes upon hearing a low growl coming from behind the brick gate. 'Sounds the same as the ones at my home,' Camelia says in a worried tone, with furrow brow appears on her forehead. Can it be the monstrous creature that appeared at my house the previous night? Are we equipped to overturn the creature since we only have ourselves as the weapon? We will try to tame and use our negotiation skills to reason with this creature. I hope this will prevail.

They run towards the brick gate, which is decorated with dahlia and daffodils bushes, and at a spur of a moment, they spot a 'werebear' in dark brown and black fur standing eight feet high, with a muscular tummy and sharp claws. It jumps over the entrance and opens his arms, and they see his arms covered with blood. It must be Lucas's! Camelia thinks. Consequently, he jumps, but the thing with his heavy body mass and giant misses and crashes down upon the brick wall.

'The beast, catch the beast!' one of the lecturers shouts.

Without hesitation, Camelia starts to chase after the creature, screaming, 'Stop! Stop! Come here, let's talk!'

It hears Camelia's words, turns its head to face Camelia, and growls loudly and fiercely to warn her to back off. As Camelia is thunderstruck, its heavy body starts to run, but the creature is too fast for Camelia to chase. She feels an intense tightening in her chest, her hands start trembling, and she is trying her best to breathe deeply for air as she feels like she's suffocating.

She lost the creature. He ran fast like a bullet train.

Why is the authority yet to arrive? 'Louise, call 911 hurry.' Camelia shouts and giving sign language at her spot and breathing deeply after a tiring chase.

A few minutes later, police and investigators come to the scene, and the college's administration notifies Lucas's parents. Investigators are appalled to see such a tragic incident. They plan for a detailed autopsy.

As for Professor Edwin and Henry, who stand steadfast like a frozen statue in the hallway, one of the police investigators touches the Professor's cheekbones, pinches his hands; however it doesn't move a muscle. Another police investigator tries to move Henry's hand to the front, trying to wake him, however, he remains still. The police investigator tries several times to push Henry and the Professor, but to no avail.

Out of the blue, a van engraved in FBI logo parks in front of the college entrance. A trolley is being used to lift both Henry and Professor Edwin into the van for further investigation. 'Hold on, Mr, could you tell me where you're taking them?' Camelia asks.

'Young girl, this will be a classified case under FBI jurisdiction; if you have any clues surrounding this incident, please don't hesitate to contact us via your college administration. Meanwhile, our researchers will conduct a detailed investigation on the ability to unfreeze both and the source of the incidents,' says the FBI.

'Excuse me Mr FBI, shouldn't there also be an interrogation session with students or lecturers? Also, shouldn't you and your team investigate the clues, foot, or handprints at the scene?'

'Let me see, are you the two ladies at the scene of the crime?' asks the FBI.

Camelia nods and asks, 'What is your name, Mr?'

'My name is Bob Sworenski; this is my card.'

'With the questions you pose, it seems to me that you

both somewhat knows more details on the tragedy: both the frozen men and the unfortunate death of the other students.'

Camelia shares everything she saw.

Bob Sworenski seems to be unimpressed when she describes the furry creature as if he believes she and Louise imagine things. But, lucky for us, Louise left her video running when we saw the creature, Camelia thinks.

The police investigator begins questioning a few students at the scene earlier than both Camelia and Louise to figure out what happened beforehand. The FBI and police investigator leave the college once the interrogations are completed.

'I hope they can find the culprit soon. I fear for the safety of all students. Also, hopefully, it relates to our family gone missing and their bizarre behaviour after returning. Sigh.. probably I should talk to Mr. FBI one day, or should we keep it to ourselves.' Camelia wonders.

***

After lectures finish, both pass by the student announcement board session so they can go to the entrance door to return to their respective homes. They see the 'Missing person' poster, where the name reads: Professor Carlos.

'We totally forgot about Professor Carlos; let's discuss these incidents with him,' Camelia suggests. She grabs Louise firmly to lead her to Professor Carlos's office. Once they reach his office door, Camelia twists the knob, and the door eventually creaks open. They enter, then close it behind them immediately to ensure no one sees them. 'Professor

Carlos, are you in your room? If you are around, please raise your pen from your desk,' Camelia says.

To her surprise, the pen rises.

'Gasp, Look! Look! The Professor is around!' Louise says excitedly.

'There were so many incidents had happened, Professor, and we need your guidance on solving these mysterious events,' says Camelia, facing the chair tucked a few metres away from the wooden desk.

Louise places a hat on the place where she thinks the Professor is sitting. 'This makes it easier for me to concentrate while talking to you,' she says.

They share the incidents with him, from the moment the ten students became like zombies until Lucas's brutal death. Since the Professor is well known for his research and deliverables, and because he won the prestigious digital and scientist award of the year (InforWorld Technology and Breakthrough prize awards), they seek his advice.

Professor writes on the paper, 'I require a specimen to find out the source of this unbecoming incidents. Camelia, since you are my top student for digital technology innovation, and Louise, I heard you are the best researcher our college has ever had, I require you both to assist me in this study.'

Camelia and Louise glance at each other and share a smile. 'We are in, Professor.'

The Professor continues, 'To prevent any suspicion, I will be in my house to do some research. My laboratory is in the basement. I am sharing with you my house keys, and this is my house address.' He writes it on a piece of paper. 'Please get sample saliva, a strain of hair/fur from all of the affected people and creatures.'

'What? You must be kidding me! How could we get hold of the monstrous fur and saliva without being badly hurt?' Camelia exclaims furiously.

'Not to mention where to find it.' Louise snatches Professor's house key from the invisible hand.

The Professor starts writing, 'You are both so intelligent, I'm sure you will find a way to gather the specimens.'

'But this is super dangerous, Professor,' Camelia's voice trembles in fear of the project they would have to undergo.

'Without the complete specimen, the findings or solutions will not be able to materialise.' Professor Carlos writes on the notepad.

Sigh. Indeed, we have no choice, Camelia thinks to herself.

'Professor, you'd better wear a wristwatch or something so we can identify you when you are at your basement during the daytime,' Camelia suggests before closing the door behind them.

***

'Okay, let's start with a plan,' Camelia suggests while they head home.

Once they reach Camelia's bedroom, she says, 'Firstly, remove all items on my study table, so we have some space to strategize. Then, let's draw our plans on this old, worn out notepad.'

'Camelia! Why are you in your room? I told you we are going to Carl's for dinner tonight, so go and get ready! And please let Louise know that tonight's dinner is for us only,' says her mother from the bottom of the stairs. 'But Mum, Louise, and I are working on a team project, so we need to have a discussion after dinner,' Camelia insists.

'My decision is final, Camelia; dinner tonight is just for us…as a family,' says her mother.

'I will call you after dinner, 'Camelia tells Louise as she gets up from her chair. From her facial expression, she is aware that Louise is annoyed since both are determined to finalise the case as soon as possible. Never before in her life had her mum not included Louise in their family dinners. They'd been like family since they were young.

There is a bang as the car door closes. 'Mum, you didn't tell me about the dinner plans earlier.' 'I message you a couple of minutes ago, young lady. Guess you didn't check your messages. She looks annoyed, pushes the car lever to D, and the car sped.

When they arrive at the diner, it's full of laughing families, the noise making it harder for Camelia to focus. Once their food shows up, within forty minutes from the timing, they order their food; Camelia notices the diner's customers gradually leave as it's already late for dinner time, leaving only the two of them and three other families.

'I have something important to tell you, Camelia.'

'What is it, Mum?' Camelia asks, with her eyes sparkling in excitement.

'I've received a promotion to Head of the Design Team,

so my work is getting more complex, and I will have many more responsibilities, which means I will be relocated to another branch.'

'That is great, and congratulations, Mum! You've been waiting for this promotion for years.' Camelia grins, filled with pride at all of her mother's hard work.

'However, Camelia, due to the distance of the location of the Headquarters, on weekdays, I will be staying close to my new office, and I will be back during the weekends to be with you.' She pauses for a moment as if gathering her words. 'I know you wouldn't want to change colleges since you are adapting very well here, and you have close friends that you can rely on as well, and you're an adult.'

'Yeah, you are right, Mum, it's better that I stay here,' Camelia says, offering her mother a smile. This will be suitable timing since I'll be busy undergoing an investigation with Professor Carlos, she thinks to herself. 'So when will you start?' Camelia asks.

'Next week Monday,' her mother says with a smile.

'Unbelievable, you only have two days to pack and find a place there?' Camelia asks.

'My office administration will provide me with a temporary lodging as part of my promotion benefits. My presence at the office is urgently needed, so I will be staying there during the weekdays to reduce our costs, so typically I only need to pack my clothes,' her mother replies.

'Good for you,' Camelia continues. 'I'm so proud of you, Mum.'

***

'Argh!' Camelia bites her fingernails, thinking, I only have tonight until Sunday to get hold of Mum's saliva and a strain of her hair for Professor Carlos's experiment.

To her surprise, her mobile vibrates beside her. 'Cam, I thought we were going to discuss the plan?' says Louise on the other end.

'Yes, we are; I will meet you first thing in the morning. Come to my house, and I will make you a mushroom and cheese omelette, 'Camelia says.

'Sounds perfect, good night,' says Louise.

At three in the morning, a strange buzzing sounds close to Camelia's ear. 'Shoo, shoo!' Camelia says and raises her hands to slap the bee. She opens one of her eyes to find the creature. Her room is still and quiet, and so she continues sleeping. Without realising what she's doing, her heavy hand manages to grab and squash the bee.' Ouch!' she cries softly as slight pain emerges from her hands. But then she continues with her sleep.

The following day when she wakes, her feet step on some debris. 'Ouch! What the heck?' says Camelia. She kneels beside her bed and checks for the debris and notices it's as though it's made from plastic with a glass-like material in a greyish colour. Guess it wasn't a bee after all, , she thinks. There are two antennas, which are broken, probably as a result of her heavy hand slapping at it. She starts smelling it for any pungent smell; just in case it is, then she will classify it as an insect. Any insect dies; it will release a pungent smell when dying. 'Strange, there is no smell. Well, I guess it's just a spy camera or a toy,' Camelia says to herself. Feeling drowsy, she doesn't contemplate, picks it up, and throws it into the dustbin next to her bed.

***

'Camelia! I'm going to the office to clear my stuff. I should be back sometime after dinner,' Camelia's mother tells her from her bedroom doorway.

'But Mum, wait for a few minutes, and let's have breakfast together. I plan to cook a mushroom cheese omelette this morning,' Camelia replies.

Her mother kisses her cheek and says, 'Thank you, sweetheart, but I have lots to pack. I will get something on the way to the office. Don't worry, I will have breakfast with you every weekend. I will not be gone forever, my girl.'

The doorbell rings and her mother casts her a smile before heading down the stairs, calling out, 'Ah, it must be Ben, I have to go now, see you tonight, young lady,' her mother says before offering her a wink. Unbelievable, work, work, and work. She feels disappointed that she is unable to have breakfast with her mum.

As the door closes behind her, Camelia heads for the staircase on the ground floor, where she sees Louise.

'Hello, let's have breakfast, and you can fill me in with the updates,' she says with a smile.

While Camelia prepares their breakfast, she explains in detail the conversation she had with her mother.

'Whoah! Why are you whispering when there is only us

here?'

'Oh, you're right,' Camelia replies.

Camelia, fearing someone is watching, strains her neck to peep through the window located at the back of the house beside the guests' room, where they'd seen the creature before.

Satisfied they're safe and alone, she starts talking in her normal tone, 'I planned to get a hold of her saliva by making breakfast and juice, but she isn't staying for any meals. I'm frustrated,' Camelia continues.

'Hmm. Let's eat. I can't think on an empty stomach,' Louise interrupts.

I have to ensure she doesn't brush, nor floss her teeth and eat nor drink thirty minutes before I take the sample. Argh! This is so difficult!' Camelia says, clenching her teeth.

'What's so difficult? When she returns tonight, you need to ensure you give her a glass of water before she goes to bed, or you have to get her to bite something that looks good but tastes bad so she won't finish it.' Louise winks. 'Plan A is good to go.'

'I was thinking about how to attract a monstrous creature who eats a human's heart to be visible, in order for us to gather its fur, etc as specimen for Professor,' Camelia thinks aloud, at the same time, her mouth is full of omelette. 'Also, not to be the victim! I have an idea; let me share it with you.' Camelia winks at her.

'I was about to check out the window at the edge of the house near to the guests' room; remember that night there was some broken glass after something hard hit the window?' Louise nods in agreement. 'The next day, the window wasn't broken at all, as though nothing had happened the previous night,' Camelia continues.

'You must be kidding,' Louise says.

'Not at all. Come on, let's check it out.

They approach the window, and Camelia touches the centre of it to gauge for any uneven materials changes, however, she is unable to find any.

Louise touches its panel, the glass, and to her surprise, nothing can be seen, nor is there any sign of fixing the broken window. 'Weird! This is a work of a genius,' exclaims Louise.

They bend down just under the window to check out for any debris or any clue for the incident or any repairs stain, however, they're both frustrated as there are none. As they get up from squatting, they can see a silhouette of a man watching with a binocular from the outside of the house; then the bushes are slightly swaying. 'Who is that?' Camelia points at the man who ran at top speed at the corner and isn't visible anymore.

A loud machine noise can be heard from the guest room, which diverts their attention.

'What about this suspiciously quiet room…the guest room… have you checked?' Louise asks Camelia.

'Nope. I didn't manage to check it as Mum is always around, suspicious of my every move,' Camelia replies.

Camelia extends her right hand to twist the door knob to the right, pushing the door, however, it doesn't budge. Camelia shakes the doorknob, and Louise touches her shoulder to stop her.

'No point shaking this door. It would be best if you had

the key,' Louise says with a grin.

'Dang, why I didn't think of that earlier?' Camelia says. In a flash, she walks toward the kitchen and, upon reaching it, peeps into a glass cabinet located above the stove. The cabinet stores neatly placed cups, plates, and saucers; also, the guest room key is in a white box located at the edge of the front row. She confidently pulls the small knob; however, it doesn't move. 'Argh! Unbelievable! She's never locked the door before this, so why now?' Camelia sighs, her irritation building.

'Let me help you,' says Louise. 'I believe I saw a tension wrench with rake kept in a drawer in the kitchen the last time I dropped by.' She takes out the tension wrench from the drawer, twists it in the right direction, then inserts the rake into the lock, and it springs open, 'Ta da! Done!' Louise says.

Stunned by her friend's help, Camelia exclaims, 'Wow, this is cool.' She can't help but smile.

Immediately she opens the box, feels the bunch of keys, and takes it out. Upon reaching the said door, she says, 'Let me see which key is for this door?' She tries one after the next. 'None of the keys fit this doorknob.' A frustrated sigh bursts from Camelia's lips. 'Guess I will have to request one from Mum once she returns,' Camelia says.

'Yeah, the top priority in our list is to get hold of what was left of Jen's clothes,' Louise says.

'I second that, with Jen's remnants clothes, we will be able to identify the causes of Jen's disappearance. I hope this clue leads us to Jen and that she's safe. We will check the guest room later as it isn't part of the plan to find the specimen.'

Once they reach Camelia's room, they notice it looks

pristinely clean. 'I haven't cleaned my room since the night Jen went missing, and now it's neat? Wait!' Camelia quickly checks her rubbish bin beside her bed and takes out the crumpled papers before finally uncovering the plastic and glass material she threw after she woke up. 'What do you think this is?' Camelia asks.

Louise walks closer to look at it. 'It seems to be a small piece of broken glass; let's try to fix it and figure it out the shape,' Louise suggests.

'This should be placed at the top, then this piece is at the side on the left, and another piece is on the right,' Louise suggests. 'How about if we do it differently, with the pointy piece at the back like a butt, the flat oblong shape piece to be placed in the centre, and the tiny curve like shape piece located at the front,' Louise says.

'Woah! Woah! It looks like a bee!' Camelia shouts excitedly.

'But why did someone send you a bee that doesn't sting?' Louise ponders.

'It looks like an oval spy camera to me. I thought I saw it somewhere in the eBay catalogue, cannot double confirm since we are not allowed to go to any application. What is the purpose of spying on me?' Camelia says.

'Bang! Bang! What is the sound? Come on, let's catch the culprit!' Camelia says and heads for her mum's bedroom. Abruptly, they pass a small window with a modern white table decorated with a vase containing a stalk of plastic lavender flowers. 'Nothing seems peculiar here,' Camelia says. Camelia signals at Louise to show her to continue walking toward her mother's bedroom and remain quiet.

Upon reaching her mother's room, they discover it's locked. Thinking quickly, Camelia takes out the bunch of keys from the kitchen cabinet downstairs and picks one or two to unlock the doorknob. 'Gotcha!' Camelia smiles. She pushes the door, which causes it to spring widely, revealing her mother's bedroom in a mess as she is busy packing. The window is slightly ajar. Upon the carpet is a book. The book is large with a leather hardcover. It seems ancient, by the crumbling pages and faded handwriting.

'This must be the one that made the loud banging noises we heard,' Louise says.

'I guess so, Louise, this book looks heavy.' Camelia turns the book's pages, and a bluish light shines from it, blinding Camelia and Louise, and immediately Camelia closes the book. 'Woah! Do you think it's the light that caused the loud banging sound? Nothing seems peculiar in this room other than this book.'

Camelia nods in agreement. Camelia picks the book with one hand, then, feeling the heaviness, observes it closely in both.

'What are you two doing in my room?' her mother snaps from the open doorway.

Camelia startles so much she accidentally drops the heavy book, and there is a loud thud as it lands on the floor.

'Out of my room, now!' Her mother's cheek is glowing red with anger, her gaze narrowed.

'Okay, sorry, Ms. Casendra,' Louise says as she walks out of the room.

Camelia's mother grabs Camelia's arms to keep her in the room. 'Hear me out, lady, no one other than you can enter my room; please respect our privacy!' Mum says sternly.

'I know, Mum! But it was an emergency, we heard a loud noise coming from your room, and both of us scampered to check it out. I was scared and thought it was a robber, so having Louise accompany me was a great help.'

'Oh, well, now I see why you look so shaken up. I'm sorry for screaming at you and your friend,' her mum says. 'Go ahead and spend time with Louise while I continue packing, and then let's have dinner together, just the two of us tonight?' her mother asks. Camelia nods in agreement and watches her mother head over to her bed.

Louise is found kneeling beside Camelia's bed when Camelia comes in and shuts her door behind her. 'Weird and emotionally unstable,' Camelia whispers to Louise. 'What did you find?'

'I'm trying to find the trace to Jen's ripped top and jeans; I couldn't find it anywhere near your wardrobe,' Louise continues. Camelia nods in agreement. 'Also, I don't recall cleaning my room since then.'

'Something fishy is going on around your house Cam,' Louise says.

'I fear for Jen's safety as she has already been missing for twenty-four hours. We cannot lodge any police report since we don't have any evidences and her mum isn't looking for her...' She sighs.

'The remnants should be somewhere in this house unless someone disposed of them. It is difficult for us to find Jen's whereabouts without the remnants, and I'm worried about her. Is she still alive? I hope no one is hurting her.' She bites her fingernails as she speaks.

***

We have dinner at Roxannes' diner nearby once mum is settled with her packing. Camelia's mother orders a plentiful of dishes mostly made from protein- there are spreads of turkey, roasted chicken, chicken casserole, beef stew, four plates of lamb shank, salmon fillet, and raw salmon. Camelia is appalled to see the variety of food being ordered and the way her mother is eating. This is the first time watching her mother eating anything other than salad. The food she ordered is fit for four to five people, not one. There must be something wrong with her metabolism if she's able to eat so much so suddenly, Camelia thinks. She gobbles up most of the food, hardly chewing it before swallowing it down. She takes the roasted chicken drumstick in one hand and the roasted turkey in the other. The table at her side is messy with what's left of the food.'It is so disgusting and embarrassing having her eating like a baby, unable to eat in a prim and proper way. This is unlike her; she often has table manners since she grew up in an elite family.

Her mother doesn't utter a word, and their table is silent besides the noise of her mother's gulping and slurping.

Looking at this, Camelia asks, 'Mum, could you slow down a bit? You're going to give yourself indigestion.'

'Excuse me, Camelia. I haven't eaten since last night,

so I'm famished,' says her mother. ' Mind your manners, my dear, you know very well I had to finalise my work in the office and packing, so I forgo my meals. I only had coffee since yesterday's breakfast.'

'Sorry, Mum, I was unaware of you skipping meals. I hope you don't do that again because it's bad for your health.'

'Do you want to say anything, Mum, since we're out for dinner?' Camelia continues. 'I thought you wanted to inform me of something before you leave.'

'Nope, I just wanted to have dinner with you outside the house since I'll be away next week. Can't we have a quiet mother and daughter dinner outing?' her mother says with a mouthful of food. 'Cam, go ahead and finish your dinner; it looks untouched. You may order other dishes if the grilled halibut fish isn't appetising.'

'Mum, you know my good friend Jen that Louise and I usually hangs out with, she is missing, and we visited her mother a few days back, she seems not to recall having Jen as her daughter. I am worried for both of them, Mum. What should I do to help them?'

'I am sorry that Jen is missing; I guess this incident is taking a toll on her mother which affects her memory. I hope that good things will come on their way soon.' mum replies. Camelia smiles at her mum.

To Camelia's disgust, her mother belches loudly with a hand on her stomach. 'Wow, finally, I am full,' her mother says. A disgusting smell from her mother's food lingers in the air. Camelia covers her mouth and nose with a napkin from the table to close her nose to avoid inhaling the smell.

'By the way, Mum, thanks for cleaning my messy room. I hope you didn't throw out any of my stuff because I couldn't find some of my items for my projects.'

'I could not stand the sight of your messy room or the stinky smell of your dirty clothes; you better be more organized when I'm not around. I don't want to hear any creepy crawlers roaming around your room.' Her mum chuckles.

CHAPTER 6

Once they're in their house, Gummy comes out of nowhere and Camelia startles.

Her mother pats, hugs, and kisses Gummy on her fluffy cheek. 'By the way, whilst I am away, Camelia you don't need to worry about taking care of Gummy because I've decided I need a companion, so I'm bringing her along with me.' Camelia smiles in relief upon hearing this. 'I know you have no time for her while I'm away.' She chuckles. 'I'll bring her home on the weekends when I'm back so you won't miss her too much.'

'Of course, Mum, it's a good idea,' Camelia says.

Once Camelia reaches her bedroom, she quickly locks her room door so her mother Casendra won't sneak into the room impromptu as she plans to investigate every inch of it for Jen's ripped clothing and any other clues as to her whereabouts.

Camelia starts to find items that eventually will lead to gathering the required specimen, going into her bathroom when she takes off her bathroom drawer to look for a box of unused latex gloves.

'Phew! Luckily I still have the stock for gloves.' Then she pulls them on and takes out the cotton tip applicators to collect traces of evidence from the shower curtain where she can see from her naked eye there is a fingerprint larger than hers. She places the cotton tip at the cotton swab box before sealing it in an envelope. Then she peers into her reading table and opens the middle drawer to keep the evidence. She changes into a new set of latex gloves to ensure accurate findings, starts moving and touching the carpet underneath her bed from back to forth, then squints as she approaches the edge of her bed, facing the wall. She blinks twice upon seeing a tiny piece of dark blue torn jeans. Determined to get hold of the evidence, she stretches herself even further with both legs raised slightly, the fingers on her right extended further. 'Argh! So close and yet so far,' Camelia pants. 'Why didn't I think of that earlier, the bamboo stick!' She gets up, takes a thin brownish bamboo stick from where it's lying against a wall beside her wardrobe. 'This will do the trick,' Camelia mutters under her breath.

In a split second, the lights switch off. 'Oh great, I was so close to getting the evidence,' Camelia says with a sigh. She backs off slightly in order to not hit her head on the bed frame. Fortunately, her mobile is in her pants pocket so she reaches out and clicks the torchlight icon.

She startles as she gets up and sees a shadow shaped like

a woman's silhouette. Could it be her mother's shadow in her room?

Camelia asks, 'Mum is that you?'

Camelia moves nearer to the shadow which stands still beside her dressing table. However, it disperses immediately when Camelia starts to walk toward it.

Then she can hear her door shackling and rattling. 'I am coming to your rescue Cam,' her mother shouts from outside Camelia's bedroom. She's wearing a pair of Nike shoes when she tries to kick the door, but it doesn't budge. 'Ouch! Then she takes the small table located beneath a window on the way to her room, pushing it from the window to Camelia's room.

'Oh my, I didn't know the table is so heavy,' Camelia's mother says under her breath. Once it reaches the front of Camelia's room door, her mother pushes hard against the door, but the force isn't enough to open it. 'Stay clear, Cam,' her mother shouts.

'OK, Mum,' Camelia says.

With a smash and a cracking noise, the door made of thick wood is finally open. 'There you are, Camelia, are you OK?' her mother asks in the darkness.

'Yes, Mum, I am,' Camelia replies. She feels like being trapped in a coffin, scared, stiff, and helpless in darkness with the silhouette of an intruder lurking in her room. Is her room safe? Hopefully, it is just the blackout and her wild imagination.

'Let's go down to the basement where the fuse box is located. Let me show you how to press the lever to get our electricity up and running,' her mother says.

While walking down to the basement, Camelia says, 'Mum, I thought I saw a shadow in my room.'

'Nonsense! It must be your imagination, a lot of things have happened. Your friend Jen is missing, and her mother is having a sudden dementia. You are definitely under a lot of stress, my girl, so please have some rest,' her mother says. 'It would be better if Louise could temporarily accompany you to sleep weekdays while I'm away until you can finally adapt to the new change. Please inform Louise of my suggestion.'

'I will, Mum. I don't think I can be left alone at the moment. Although she whispers to herself in her heart, with the few incidents happening, I feel more secure having someone to accompany me, especially at night.

***

The clock strikes one in the morning, and Camelia's mobile alarm rings, waking her up sharply since she plans to gather Casendra's hair from her hairbrush for a specimen. She tiptoes toward her mum's bedroom, ensuring she does not make any sound. Upon reaching, she finds her room door is left ajar, so easily for Camelia to creep into her room. Once she enters, she notices her room is still messy with documents lying on two bedside tables.

Then she creeps toward her toilet in order not to make any sound and pushes the door inch by inch without switching on any of the lights. Once she enters, she closes the door behind her and switches on her small pocket torch for vision. Initially, she skims through the items on the sink, however, there are no brushes to be found. Then she notices there are three drawers on each side of the sink, so she opens the top drawer to search for the hairbrush. With the dim light of her pocket torchlight, it assists Camelia in searching between the drawers, and upon reaching the right-side drawer, there are two hairbrushes kept in it, both full of her mother's hair. Camelia smiles to herself. Without wasting any time, she manages to take a strain or two of Casendra's hair with her right hand wearing the latex glove and gently places it into the airtight plastic bag. Quickly she places it into the pocket of her pyjamas.

Out of the blue, her mother appears in the toilet with the lights on, and Camelia knows she's been caught. 'What are you doing in my toilet without any lights? her mother says between yawns.

'My toothpaste just finished, and I went to sleep without brushing my teeth. I came here to take yours, but I didn't want to disturb you, so I didn't switch on the lights.'

Her mother's expression softens. 'OK, go ahead and get my toothpaste, but please get some sleep after brushing your teeth,' her mother says.

Camelia slips the hair specimen into her backpack zipper on the left as she enters her bedroom and goes straight to bed.

***

The alarm rings early, and Camelia gets up with lots of energy as she's eager to prepare breakfast for her mother, and it's the last day for her to be together with her mum.

She takes out oranges and celery from the fridge, cuts and squishes them into the juice blender to make a healthy juice for her mum. The juice is ready in good time as her mother appears in the kitchen.

'I have last minute packing at the office, I will be back for lunch,' her mother says.

'Why not drink your juice first, for strength? It isn't often your lovely daughter makes it for you,' Camelia says while handing the juice over.

'No thanks, I will grab something on the way, and I cannot drink orange juice on an empty stomach,' her mother says.

Camelia starts to hunch and sigh. Off she goes again, leaving Camelia feeling disappointed since she just wants to spend time with her mother and get her saliva specimen. Another fail attempt. Guess I will try another time tonight.

***

'Now is the time to finalise the search for Jen's specimen,' Camelia whispers to herself. But a sound from upstairs interrupts her thoughts. She quickly takes a long dark blue umbrella as a defence tool, texts Louise then quietly climbs the staircase.

Thud. Thud. Thud. The sound resonates.

'Who is there? I will call the police this instant,' Camelia shouts. The sound stops as she speaks. But the sound changes, becoming a rattling, like someone is playing a traditional drum. Once Camelia reaches the last staircase, it grows louder, and Camelia realises it's coming from her mother's bedroom. As Camelia reaches the bedroom, about to turn the doorknob, the sound suddenly stops, and the house grows completely still.

Within a minute or so, the rattling and clattering sound resumes.

Camelia's heart skips a beat and with her hands trembling, due to her curiosity, she opens the door. As she steps into the room, it's still, quiet, and in darkness. Camelia walks further into the centre of the room, curious to find the source of the sound.

Firstly, she walks toward her mother's luggage located on a long stool in front of the bed frame, where she discovers the luggage is open with full of folded clothing. 'Nothing weird here,' Camelia says to herself. As she turns her head, now facing the window, she sees the heavy book on top of a table below the window and notices it's glowing with a strange blueish light. It has a diamond symbol at the centre. She can't remember where she's seen it before but it's familiar.

'Gotcha!' her mother says.

'Urgh!' Camelia exclaims in surprise that her mum is already at home.

'Cam, my dear, I don't understand why you are so attracted to my reading desk,, but you are in my room a lot these days. What's going on with you?' her mother says.

Camelia turns her head to look at the desk again.

'But Mum, I thought I heard a drumming sound coming from your bedroom, and there was a huge ancient book on your desk!' Camelia says.

Her mother laughs at her. 'You and your wild imagination, now you make me worry whether I can leave you alone in this house and if you will be safe. I have informed Mrs Elliot, our neighbour, to look out for you. This is my new office phone number and my apartment address just in case you need to reach me in an emergency,' her mother continues.

'I will keep your office number safe. Don't worry about me, Mum; I'm an adult and fit to stay home by myself."

***

Camelia returns to her room and, in due course, checks the corner of her bed frame for the dark blue tattered cloth she saw last night. As she kneels and digs her head underneath her bed frame, she is caught by surprise to learn that the tattered cloth isn't visible. She texts Louise to update her on the findings.

`Cam, what on earth are you searching for?' her mother asks.

'Oh, Louise said the nut of her earring went missing, and she thinks it may have rolled down onto my bedroom carpet when she came over yesterday,' Camelia explains.

'Let Louise come tomorrow and let her find it herself, my dear,' her mother says with a smile. 'Let's go down for dinner; I bought some takeaways on the way home from the office.'

Camelia asks, 'What is it you felt when you were outside for a meeting that day when Ben, your assistant, was worried sick that you and other colleagues went missing?' Camelia asks.

'There you go again about that day. We were busy discussing a project with our new prospective client, who is over demanding that r our graphic design includes nature stuff,' her mother replies.

Thinking quickly, Camelia places her mother's favourite glass on the table, filled with natural water. Clearly, her mother is thirsty because she drains the water in only a few seconds. 'Let me refill for you, Mum,' Camelia says.

Her mum is about to object it when her mobile rings, so she signals a nod of agreement to Cam's suggestion. While her mother walks away from the dining table to talk, Camelia takes the opportunity to take out a cotton tip she kept in her jacket's pocket next she scores the tip onto the glass where the spot of her mother's saliva is located. A few minutes later, she realised no longer hear her mother's voice, feeling panic that she may suddenly appear, so she places it into a cotton swab box in an instant. The box is slightly dented since it is kept in a confined space in her jacket pocket. Suddenly, she sees the reflection of her mother via the cabinet, which it's door made from glass located beside the water cooler. In order not to be caught, she slips the box under the tablecloth beside the cooler.

'You look tired, Mum, with the packing; let me do the dishes, and you should get some sleep early,' Camelia says.

'You are right, Cam.'

Once her mother is upstairs, Camelia texts Louise, Mission A accomplished.

CHAPTER 7

'Hello, this is Ms. Lai from the college administration speaking, are Camelia and Louise on the line, please?'

'Hi, it's Camelia here.'

'This is regarding the recent tragedy in college i.e Lucas, Henry, and Professor Edwin; since both of you were at the scene and have video footage on the tragedy, the college administration has decided to appoint both of you to the team of investigators. Therefore, I need both of you to go to Moonsriver town police station right now.'

'Okay,' Camelia replies. 'We will be there soon.'

An hour or so later, they reach the police station, and Ms. Lai is at the lobby greeting them. Then they are taken to see the FBI officer Bob, who explains, 'We will begin our intense research and investigation, as you will be appointed as the team members,' Bob says.

Ms. Lai continues; 'Please give full cooperation with

the FBI on this investigation and ensure confidentiality, no preliminary investigation to be divulged to anyone. All investigations and specimens are to remain within these four walls. Got it, girls?

Camelia and Louise nod at Ms. Lai.

'You will be working hand in hand with our best scientists in the FBI, Dr. David Tzo and Dr. Alicia Scwerzerzof.' Beside him, they exchange nods and smiles.

'We are speechless and honored to be part of the team; however, will it affect our lectures?' Louise asks Ms. Lai.

'We will inform the college Principle and Ms. Lai of any findings or investigation activity that we require from both of you for the week or the day itself,' Bob interrupts Ms. Lai while showing them both to a discreet room. He presses several numbers on a touchpad situated beside the steel doors, and once they step in, within a few feet from the entrance are the frozen bodies of Henry and Professor Edwin.

Camelia and Louise remain standing still, the colour of their skin changing to copper. Henry's eyes open widely, looking shocked, whereas the Professor's eyes are covered by his left hand.

Camelia touches it and exclaims, 'Wow, the texture that turns them is hard, cold, and a knocking sounds hollow as though they have turned to a thin sheet of metal.'

Dr. David explains, 'We've tried a lot of melting point apparatus like the Thiele tube to determine the melting point of both of them, and radiation to melt or rearrange the neutron but to no avail.'

Interesting. The doctors are trying to dissolve them by mixing chemical liquid and rearranging the neutron numbers within their bodies. In other words, they are trying to use some chemicals to melt them. I hope it will work soon. Camelia thinks.

'Each time we try to melt them, their heartbeat stops, therefore we have to abruptly stop our experiment to revive them,' Dr. Alicia interrupts. 'However, both heartbeats are sometimes normal, and sometimes they beat faster as though something is bothering them inside.'

'It's dangerous to their heart since the pressure of using different electrons may serve an electric shock which will be detrimental to their hearts,' Louise whispers to Camelia.

'As for Lucas's corpse, we found traces of a bear-like bite with a razor-sharp six-inch deep cut in the centre of his chest, and the creature I would say left a symbol at his neck,' Bob continues.

Camelia steps closer, examining the corpse, 'I've seen this symbol before! But I can't remember where I noticed it.'

Upon hearing Camelia's words, Bob says, 'Please let us know once you remember so we can have an extensive investigation. Thanks for your time, ladies; we will be in touch.'

***

The expected night arrives. The doorbell rings several times as the twenty college students gather at Camelia's house.

The noise from the crowds slams through Camelia's house as the students drink and dance. 'Freak man, this house is cool; I like the gardens the most,' one of the students exclaims loudly.

Camelia has always been proud of her home and its two thousand square foot garden terrace with a modern umbrella table and chairs for her guests to seat, so she smiles at the compliment. For this party, she orders pizzas, beef/ chicken burgers, a variety of salads, and different types of vodka are placed at the table. The lights are dimly lit inside the house to encourage students to mingle and party outside. She is excited that there was more turnout than expected, especially being a top student nerd.

Feeling butterflies in her stomach at the thought of the monstrous creature she and Louise will have to face; fine lines are visible on her forehead as she is thinking of ways to chase the monstrous creature without being eaten. Also, the added responsibility of keeping everyone alive.

A few days before the event, Camelia manages to persuade Ahmed, the college's top music student, to be a DJ for the night. He came with his music instruments, set it up since afternoon and has been practicing before the event. Students like the music he picks, plays, and how he entertains the party. A lot of upbeat music is being played, which puts her guests in the mood to dance from the living room into the garden.

Within an hour, Camelia announces, 'Hi everyone, I hope all are having fun, as you know this is a get to know each other party, so we will be having a 'wink murder' game soon. Please come to the garden yard for those who would like to play,' Camelia says via the microphone.

'Alright, count me in dude.'

'This game sounds interesting; I am in too,' another

student replies.

'Let me count… fifteen people altogether; that's a good number to get the ball rolling,' Camelia continues. 'The rule of the game is that all players must close their eyes; I will tap one person on the shoulder and appoint them as the murderer. All others are detectives; therefore, you are required to hide within the compound of my house. The murderer will find one by one, consequently, once the murderer finds a player, he or she will wink at you, and you have to pretend to be dead in a tragic way. The winners are those who are artistic enough in their acts of death.'

'Woohoo. That is cool, I am so in!' cries out Tom, the most sought-after guy in the college wearing an unbuttoned shirt with yellow Bermuda shorts. He quickly kisses Alexia on her lips. She shakily lifts her arms to wrap around his neck, pushing her curvy body against his muscular one. Then Tom's tongue darts out to trace her bottom lip, and she releases a moan. After that, they continue drinking vodka in another hand and laughing loudly.

'Oh, so disgusting, yikes,' Camelia says to herself.

'Let's the game begin, one, two, three, .ten… All fifteen people, please shut your eyes, no peeping.' Camelia taps on Zoe's shoulder. The petite blonde girl is appointed as the wink murderer and has to pretend to hide along with others in order not to disclose her identity. 'Now it's hiding time; I'll count up to forty for everyone to hide within the counting timeframe.'

Go! Go! Before the wink murderer captures you,' Camelia says jokingly.

While Camelia is busy entertaining guests, Louise has a vital role in attracting the creature. She pours a litre of goat blood, ordered from a nearby butcher that morning, on the ground at one of the garden tables with a pound of raw meat. Camelia hopes these will attract the monstrous creature.

Whilst Louise is attracting the creature; Camelia is busy coordinating her party. There is a couple hiding behind bushes of chrysanthemum flowers in the garden, hugging each other. Another couple is hiding in the kitchen underneath the dining table, covering them with a long white lace table cloth. Next, the couples moved upstairs to hide in Camelia's mother's room, and others hide in the dining and living room.

'Everybody ready, the appointed murder will begin to catch you,' Camelia says via the microphone. Zoe steps into the house via the ajar garden door; she walks silently, barefooted ; crouching slightly to ensure balance, and a slight sound of the wooden floor can be heard.

Camelia follows her as she is the lead in organising and a referee.

Subsequently, Zoe and Camelia place their foot on another spot, and to their relief no sound is made. They try to maintain their balance by bending their knees and continuing a crouching position to reach the living room. Getting inside the living room, they both see the reflection of a couple, one wearing a yellow top and another wearing a red cap hiding behind an antique cabinet with neat stacks of books. Camelia watches Zoe smile to herself; she must be clearly thinking, 'This is easy,' as she creeps closer to the couple, winks, and says, 'Gotcha!' The couple's eyes open wide in surprise. One instantly pretends they have been struck by lightning and falls onto the floor, pretending to be dead. 'Good job, I'm going for the next victim,' Zoe says.

Then Camelia, the event organiser of the game, comes to take a photo of the pretend tragic death in the living room.

Next, Zoe walks slowly, facing the staircase direction, and this time there is no creaking sound since all steps are covered with stair runners made of natural fibre in a dark maroon colour. She quickens her steps to search for another couple, with Camelia dawdle at her back. Upon reaching the second floor, she tries to open Camelia's bedroom door, but it's locked, so she proceeds to walk further in. She passes a window with a transparent bluish curtain with a small desk decorated with a vase. They hear both Vanessa and James's voices coming from Casendra's room. Camelia turns the doorknob; however, it doesn't budge open. Camelia notices a CCTV monitor placed on the wall beside her mum's room door.

'Why didn't I think of this before?' Camelia feels annoyed with herself. She quickly switches on the monitor, and when Zoe sees this, she stops pushing the doorknob, and they watch what is happening inside the locked room.

They view the couple named Vanessa and Jamie busy chit-chatting and giggling, until they hear a thud, and Jamie whispers in Vanessa's ear, 'Shush… let's go and hide.'

They watch them skimming the room for a space to hide. Vanessa signals to Jamie, saying she will be hiding in the toilet, and tiptoes toward the toilet, drawing the bathtub curtain, step into it, and closes it. Then Jamie creeps into the cupboard just a few steps away from the bed where both were seated, opens the door, blinks upon seeing many clothes hanging, skims with his eyes from left to the centre, and finds a space on the furthest right.

The thumping sound grows louder. Camelia's heart thumps when she hears the sound. Then both watch Jamie crawling into the cupboard, closer to the space where many coats and dresses are hanging neatly together. The length and thickness of the coat's material cover him much better. Jamie and Vanessa stay silent even as they hear the thudding sound resonating through the room.

He hears a screeching shrieking sound; then it stops for a moment before echoing this time in a high-frequency sound. Camelia gasps. This sound is similar to the one Camelia heard before.

Sweat trickles down Camelia's forehead, and Camelia's hands start to tremble. There are two CCTV; one facing Mum's closet from the opposite of the window, another facing from her bed toward her bathroom; this is the location of her safe box where her mother keeps her valuables.

Suddenly, the room falls silent. Camelia and Zoe notice that Jamie appears more confident once the sound has died away and lets go of the dresses covering his ears. Out of the blue, they are shocked to witness a huge bulky hand wrapping around his neck when suddenly the attacker's elbow goes under Jamie's chin with his bicep, and his forearm is wrapped around his neck. Then the attacker tightens their grip and pushes Jamie's head forward with his other arm. Jamie gasps for air, hitting and pulling the attacker's hands, but his face becomes pale, and the hands at his throat are too strong. He gasps for air. Jamie gets up, his legs kicking mid-air, struggling to break free from the attacker's grip when he suddenly manages to stop the intruder temporarily. The intruder is fast to react, catches Jamie off guard, and abruptly places a knife on his neck. Jamie's blood drips down his neck…

Upon seeing the brutal fight, impromptu Zoe knocks on the door repeatedly to distract the intruder. While Camelia tries to break the door by pushing the small table against the door, however to no avail.

At the garden terrace, Louise is panting and sweating since it's summer and there's no breeze to cool herself. She's still waiting impatiently for the creature to arrive; however, she's furious since she's been alone with the ghastly smell of blood for thirty minutes, but there seems to be no sign of any creatures lurking in the garden. As it strikes midnight, the night remains quiet, all music switched off, and the DJ has returned.

Upstairs, Camelia watches Zoe manages to use a pin to free the doorknob, opens the door cautiously, and screams,' Urgh! That smell is disgusting!' They enter, their eyes staring into the darkness. Camelia switches her mobile torchlight on and walks further into the room, where there is the sound of someone falling in the bathroom, forcing both to spin around. They hear a scream from downstairs as they are about to approach it. Camelia stops walking inward instead runs out from the room as the shout turns to an eerie shrieking sound. 'Zoe, please check on Jamie and Vanessa while I check out downstairs.'

Goosebumps start to appear on her hands. She swallows her saliva and breathes deeply to regain her confidence. *Oh my, our target has arrived: the monstrous creature. I must find Louise, as she alone won't be able to overturn the creature,* Camelia thinks.

According to Louise iMessage Camelia, a few minutes ago, she initially attempted to attract the creature with only goat blood; however, it was a failure. Therefore, she informed that she will cut herself to release her fresh blood, mixing it into the goat blood and meat. She suggested that the smell of the mixture will attract the enormous furry creature. Camelia smiles to herself. Her suggestion works perfectly; the mixture attracts it, the creature is coming from the direction of the community park, and Camelia watches as it jumps as high as fifteen feet. His enormous body crashes onto the wooden garden table, seeking the raw meat mixed with goat and Louise's blood. The table is broken into halves as the table cannot withhold the weight and the impact of the creature. He gobbles up the meat noisily and slurps the blood.

The terrifying creature is still hungry and must be able to smell the source of fresh blood coming from Louise, Camelia realises. Upon seeing this, Camelia runs at full speed in Louise's direction. Panting with her heart rate rising, Camelia manages to pull a stunned Louise down by the waist, and they hide behind the thick dark brown wooden portable barbecue grille table in the nick of time before the huge creature jumps high. It crashes onto the next wooden garden table where Louise is standing, frozen still.

Camelia notices the odour of fresh human blood entices

the creature, so in order to deviate his attention, she runs a metre away from Louise, standing beside a row of bushes and big vases of flowers, and takes a penknife to slide a deep cut in her left hand, crying out as her blood drips. 'Come here! Come here, you ugly beast!' Then she tears off a part of her t-shirt and wraps it with her blood to entice the creature.

Camelia continues shouting and waving her hands at the beast. While waiting for the creature to come, she notices the skewers that have been placed on the burner; one is placed with the bloody torn t-shirt, while she holds another in her hands as a makeshift weapon. Finally, the creature turns to face her, its bold eyes fixed on the wound on her hand, and runs at top speed, even though its body is heavy and covered with fur. As the creature nears her spot, she extends the skewer with the blood-stained remains and holds it up in the air to attract it.

Once the creature arrives at her side, she pierces its left arm with the skewer, forcing it to growl in pain. Then, Camelia starts twisting the skewers to scarp its fur for Professor Carlos's specimen. However, to no avail, since the skewers isn't meant to scrap, so no fur comes off with the scraping, and instead, there are only scratches on its skin.

Louise, who finally reaches her after running from the garden veranda, takes the long barbecue steel scissors from the table beside them. She stretches her hands to be at a distance from the creature, fearing the thought of it jumping on her, and she starts snipping his fur. As the scissors manage to cut the tip of its fur, it falls onto the ground. The 'were bear' raises its paws high with its heavy feet stomping on the ground, then it slaps the wooden garden table beside it, which causes the garden chairs to fling high up and fall on the driveway nearby with a crash.

At the same time, Camelia is blown away by the strong impact. 'Ouch!' she says. When she falls into the bushes at the side garden, bruises and some deep scratches are visible on her skin. It's the same beast as the ones lurking in her room, Camelia realises, spotting Jen's pink ribbon tied at the back of his furry neck.

A couple hiding for the wink murderer games shiver in fear before scampering into the house to hide under the thick cloth placed on top of the kitchen table.

With deep determination to get more fur, Camelia resumes her chase after the creature. She runs full speed toward the garden porch beside her garden terrace and takes an umbrella from the pavement before entering her house. She shovels the pointed umbrella at the creature and stabs it with the tip, trying to distract it.

Louise runs and reaches timely to snip its fur, and it drops onto the grass; the creature seems annoyed and releases a heavy growl. Then it looks at Camelia with its red ruby eyes before scrambling into the house.

Louise, who is standing next to Camelia, says, 'Let's chase after it; it will destroy your house if we don't.' Her face looks alarmed with her eyes wide open, momentarily freezing at the thought of her house being ransacked by the beast. 'Let's chase after him quickly!'

The creature scampers quickly into the kitchen, pushing furniture over on its way, sending chairs tumbling onto the floor and breaking vases in the process. Clearly still hungry, it places its heavy paw underneath the table, trying its luck to get hold of some human flesh, and consequently pulls at a lady's leg from her hiding spot underneath the table. Fortunately for her, she's wearing a pair of three-inch black leather boots, so its sharp claws only manage to pierce the leather. But it pulls and pulls at the lady's leg, inch by inch, and the lady screams at the top of her voice, trying to pull her leg away from the firm grip. She's unable to do so and grabs hold of the tablecloth, pulling it bit by bit to pull herself further inside the table. As she stretches, plates and glasses come crashing toward her, but she grabs a few of them and smacks them against the creature's large head…

Camelia gasps at this sight. Sweat trickle at the back of her neck as she's shivering, wondering how she can help her mate. Louise whispers that she should take the golf stick from the blue vase to distract him. Camelia does as her friend suggests, grinding the stick against the floor to try to distract the beast.

The creature momentarily stops grabbing her leg and shoe due to the sudden blow, turns to face Camelia, and the distraction gives the girl an opportunity to climb to her feet. As she's bending in the crawling position, trying to balance herself to wake up, in a blink of the eye, he tries to grab hold of the lady, and the lady falls onto the floor, hitting her head on the floor…bleeding and falling unconscious. Camelia inches nearer to the beast then hits him with the golf stick, but the creature doesn't seem fazed by the golf stick. Louise throws the plates and glasses on the floor to distract him. But the creature ignores it and quickly grabs the fresh heart. He instantly gobbles it.

While he's eating, a couple still hides under the table, frozen in panic. Camelia and Louise wave at them, frantically pointing at them to move out from under the table. But before they can move even an inch, the creature takes its prey once again.

The two people underneath the table scream when it reaches for a leg, then turn their heads without realising, and both come to face it. The two people start to realise they must escape after being frozen still for some time, and the creature's paws become slippery as one of the couples pour water on it. Both start to get up and run as fast as their feet can bring them towards the kitchen door, but the door is locked. The man shakes the doorknob, but it still doesn't budge open.

With her hands trembling, Camelia takes the blue vase located next to the staircase, throws it in the creature's direction, and it misses him however, the bits and pieces of the broken glasses from the vase manage to hit the creature in its right paw. Since it's a small piece, the creature doesn't seem affected by it, and the creature snatches one of them in one arm by pulling her waist; its claws are so thick and sharp they cause the skin to bleed.

The creature breaks the other side of the lady's hands, slicing off her flesh, placing its sharp claws into it, grabbing and opening its large mouth, and placing it inside. It starts wiping its mouth with its furry paw. Whilst doing this, a ray of sunlight comes in through the kitchen window, blinding the creature slightly, and it starts rubbing its eyes to avoid the sun. Camelia and Louise pant, and Camelia feels nausea as they watch in horror, their college friend died in front of their eyes, her blood flowing with her torn flesh and arms gone, and an empty hole in the centre of the corpse.

Downstairs at the edge of the scene, Zoe cries out loudly in fear. Camelia sneaks out from her hiding place, places an arm around her waist, then gives her a hug for comfort. 'Cam, you'd better look at Jamie and Vanessa,' Zoe stammers.

'Let's check on both Jamie and Vanessa,' Camelia says to Louise.

'Please call 911 while we go upstairs to check them out,' Louise instructs Zoe.

They climb the staircase; Camelia is aware of the events that happened to Jamie, breathes deeply with hands trembling, thinking of the reality she will see once she opens the door. But, before reaching her mother's bedroom, she whispers to Louise, 'Jamie was brutally killed, but I'm not sure about Vanessa.'

Hearing this, Louise's eyes open wide. Once they reach Camelia's mother's bedroom, they see that the door is left ajar, and the room is in pitch darkness. Then Camelia steps a foot inside as a thumping sound appears, stunning them. She steps further in, a glowing yellow light shining from the direction of the table, where it's located underneath the window, opposite the door. Suddenly, Camelia feels butterflies in her stomach, curious and fearful of the next event. She inches further into the room, the light sufficient for her to see her steps, and as she reaches the centre of the bedroom, four lights in a diamond shape appear from the leather, heavy-looking book.

Camelia gasps and smiles. 'It's the same symbol on the neck of Lucas's corpse.

'Unbelievable!'

Then Louise comes in noisily and exclaims, 'Ew! This room is smelly. Yikes!'

The symbol immediately disappears, leaving Camelia puzzled.

She switches on the lights. Camelia turns her head to face Louise. 'Did you see that?" Camelia asks.

'Nope, I only saw you staring at the window. I thought you were dreaming,' Louise replies in an annoying tone.

'Can we be in a hurry to find those two friends before the police and ambulance arrives?'

'Let's go to the cupboard first, where I and Zoe saw Jamie's murder. I would like to see it again.'

Camelia takes the lead, and upon reaching the cupboard, Louise closes her mouth to prevent her from screaming. 'It's Jamie; his eyes open wide, his face looks pale blue, he must be trapped, entangled within Casendra's coats, belts and scarves?' she asks.

'We saw a bulky, hairy hand squeezing his neck; he must have struggled to save himself, it worsens, the items or the murderer must have choked him to death,' Camelia says.

'Look. Belts and scarves are covered with bloody dots here and there covering his neck,' Louise says.

'It doesn't look like they strangled him,' Camelia says while Louise takes a photo of Jamie's injured neck.

'Next, the bathroom to check on Vanessa, we didn't notice her via the CCTV monitor, I fear for her safety after seeing the fate of Jamie. Would you like to accompany me over there?'

Camelia asks Louise in a whisper. Louise nods, and upon reaching the bathroom, she pushes the door is sounds' creak'; the pungent smell is released into the air as she walks into the bathroom. Camelia feels the urge to vomit, instantly covering her nose with her sleeve. 'Now that is better,' Camelia mutters under her breath. Then her hands grapple the toilet wall to find a switch. 'Got it.' She switches on the lights, and she can feel her heartbeat pounding faster as she makes her way over to the bathtub.

Camelia bites her index finger as she draws the shower curtain aside, her mouth and eyes open wide in surprise when she sees a body in the bathtub, brutally scarred with flesh here and there like a butcher had cut it. Her hands are chopped off its body; there is a hole in the heart and a yellow mini skirt draped on its bottom. The bathtub is semi-filled with human blood. Louise, who is standing beside her, screams under her breath in fear of the attacker.

Suddenly, they feel a sudden blow to their heads, and the darkness overwhelms them.

***

A ray of lights coming from the direction of the window light up Camelia's eyes, and she rubs them. 'What?' She jolts up, recalling the incident as it's fresh in her mind, and turns her face to the left, feeling relief when she spots Louise beside her in her purple polka-dot pyjamas.

'Wake up! Come on!' Camelia says.

'What! I'm still sleepy; it's Saturday; why do we need to be in a hurry?' Louise replies in a sleepy voice.

'Don't you remember what happened last night at my house party? The bloody deaths and the monstrous creature on my garden terrace?' Camelia says.

'Yes, it is fresh in my mind. Ouch, my head hurts. Oh no! My head feels bumpy on the right side… it's swollen!' Louise shouts.

'Lazy bum, get ready quickly. Let's search the house,' Camelia says. Seeing Louise closes her eyes, Camelia shakes Louise's body to wake her more quickly. 'Alright, I am awake.' Louise gets up while rubbing her eyes.

CHAPTER 8

After getting ready and climbing down the staircase, they smell the delicious aroma of sausages, and once their feet touch the downstairs floor, they turn their heads in the direction of the smell. It's coming from the kitchen table. Therefore, they walk into the kitchen and see her mum's silhouette facing the kitchen sink.

'Mum, when did you arrive?' Camelia asks excitedly.

'Cam, I've been at home since yesterday morning. As I promised when I took this promotion, I'm home with you on Saturdays and Sundays,' her mother says. 'You were both so tired after playing frieze ball with Gummy and the neighbour's dog, Coco. Both of you accidentally hit your heads on the side table at the garden terrace. You were unconscious, so I brought you both to the clinic nearby. Phew! Luckily both of you were semi-conscious by the time we got into the clinic, and the doctor gave me this medication for the pain and healing,' her mother says whilst giving them the medication. 'Please take it promptly twice a day, both of you, for at least a week.'

Camelia and Louise glance at each other, equally appalled by the turn of events.

'Have a seat and divulge into my breakfast cooking. It smells good, right?'

They smile in return, pull off the chairs, and slowly move to the chairs, where they start taking the sausages and baked beans.

Whilst both sitting down side by side for breakfast, Louise pushes the tablecloth pretending to straighten it; however, her eyes are glancing around for any blood stains or tears resulting from last night's event. However, she finds nothing. She feels puzzling; her forehead shows lines of confusion, she starts to fidget as she is confused by the turn of events.

Seeing Louise's facial expressions, Camelia feels disbelief in their findings and adamantly wants to see for herself. She accidentally drops her knife on the floor and uses her feet to push it underneath the table. 'Oh my, clumsy me, let me go down and pick it up,' Camelia says. Suddenly she bends down and crawls further inward, pretending to get ahold of her knife while at the same time looking for any clues of the last night's incident like bloodstains; however, there is no luck.

'Camelia, get up. Your breakfast will go cold,' her mother says.

'Got it!' Camelia slowly retracts her crawl by reversing herself bit by bit, her eyes wandering end to end of the underneath table, unable to see anything strange. Then as she's about to get up from her bending position, she leans closer to the tablecloth, pretending it touches her nose and smells the aroma of lavender of the fresh soap washed by it. Surprisingly, the tablecloth doesn't smell like blood. Strange…the tablecloth smells nice. Was it washed? As she's about to get out from the table, she spots her mother's long pleated skirt. Camelia turns to face her mother, and whilst getting up, she notices the woman's lips tighten, the corner of her mouth point downwards, her eyebrows lower, and she crosses her arms.

'Girl, what are you doing? Go and get a new knife and finish your breakfast; I'm going to get something at the Department store. After that, I will have dinner with you.' Her mother's tone is firm.

After her mother has left, Camelia hears her car exhaust vroom, which confirms she's away, and the two girls hastily run upstairs toward her mother's bedroom.

Camelia turns the doorknob, and surprisingly it's easy as it isn't locked this time. She pushes the door open, steps inside, opening the door wider for Louise to enter.

'My God, this room looks clean and tidy and smells like rose air freshener,' Louise says.

'Surprisingly, you are right; there is no blood or butcher corpse smell here, either.'

Concerned after her mother's previous sudden appearance, without wasting any time, Camelia closes the door behind her, locks it inside, her heart beat accelerating faster than usual. Her muscles feel tense as she heads for her mother's cupboard. Louise follows quickly behind her. Camelia places her hands onto the cupboard handle, breathes in, and reminds herself to remain calm. She pulls the handle and the door open, and an aroma of rose evaporates into the air. She opens the door wider, revealing her dresses, coats, scarves, and belts neatly placed on the hangers.

Both look at each other in disbelief.

Louise, who clearly isn't satisfied with the findings, comes forward to stand side by side with Camelia, then bends down and starts smelling for any traces of blood or the corpses of Jamie. Or even any traces of his clothes.

'This cannot be it. Jamie must be hidden somewhere.'

Instantly, she reaches the back of the cupboard, moving from the furthest left, then to the middle, and then to the end of the cupboard.

Camelia whispers, 'What are you doing?'

'Maybe there is an opening to hide or a passage to throw the corpses into,' Louise says. She presses the back of the cupboard harder in case there's a latch to release the back of the cupboard; however, it's intact, and no holes are detected. 'This is very weird; everything looks normal this morning,' Louise says.

'Let's search the bathroom for Vanessa,' Louise says.

Camelia pushes the door open wide, and the bathroom smell aroma of rose air freshener lingers in the air. 'Let me see what's behind the shower curtain,' Camelia says while inhaling deeply since her anxiety is becoming overwhelming. But she manages to pull aside the shower curtain.

They stare, open-mouthed, at an empty bathtub, astounded there's no sign of a lady's body being minced like meat with its heart out in the bathtub. Could anyone have easily disposed of the bodies within such a short time frame?

Camelia asks herself.

'Do you see what I see, Camelia? Whatever happened last night has disappeared, or are we drugged to think creatures and bodies are brutally murdered?' Louise says.

'Let's double confirm by looking at the garden terrace,' Camelia suggests. But the barbecue table set isn't perturbed, and the wooden garden table looks intact and neat with no scratches. Camelia touches the centre of the table to ensure the damages haven't been repaired overnight.

'Nope, everything is in perfect condition,' Camelia says. 'Wait, what about the creature's fur? I snipped at the tip, and it fell onto the grass around this spot, if I recall correctly.'

Louise bends down, unable to see with her naked eye, takes out her magnifying glasses from her jacket pocket and uses them to search for the fur on the neatly cut grass. She crawls inch by inch, then moves further aside to the next table. 'I found it; this is the one, right?' Louise says. 'Yes! Yes!' Louise lowers her voice. 'I guess there is a mastermind that wanted us to look crazy; we must investigate this,' Louise continues.

Is this the same mastermind as those who zapped the ten students who went weird along with Professor Carlos? I wonder if there's another culprit behind the creation of the creature as well as Henry and Professor Edwin frozen, Camelia thinks aloud.

'Got it! Why not visit Mr. Bucket, my neighbour, to see if he heard anything last night? Also, as Mum said, we played with his dog until we faced with injury, why not take the opportunity to find out whether we played with his dog

Coco?'

'Hello, is there anyone home?' Camelia asks as she knocks on the door. When there is no response, she presses the bell located on the left panel of the front door.

'Who is there?' a man's voice shouts.

'It's me, Camelia, your neighbour,' Camelia says.

The door is slightly open. 'I'm not feeling well. Can you come back tomorrow?'

'We won't not be long, Mr. Bucket, please allow us in for a few minutes; this is crucial,' Camelia pleads.

'Alright girl, come on in, I see you are bringing a fine lady with you; I like visitors as beautiful as her,' Mr. Bucket winking to show both that he is kidding.

Louise and Camelia smile in return, and walk into the house, closing the door behind them.

Coco barks and Mr. Bucket scalds him, 'Shh, Coco, they are our neighbours. Be kind to them; this isn't how we to treat our neighbours. 'Come on into my living room and have a seat. I haven't had any visitors ever since my dear wife Rosy passed away.'

'You do have a cosy house, Mr. Bucket, and we are sorry on the demise of Mrs. Rosy,' Camelia continues. 'May we know when she passed away, and what caused it?'

'Not at all, she passed away ten years ago; she transmitted a weird disease after she took care of a patient in the military hospital, as she was a dedicated and caring nurse,' Mr. Bucket continues. He smiles as he describes his late wife.

'I am sure she was,' Camelia says.

'So what can I do for you, young ladies?' Mr. Bucket asks.

'We are just dropping in to check out whether you are okay. Did you hear any strange noises last night?' Louise impatiently interrupts.

'Let me think. What did I do?' His left hand pats Coco; another hand strokes his white beard as he ponders the question. 'It was quite a peaceful night with the normal cricket sound; I was on my wooden rocking chair in front of my television set watching my favourite soccer game. I have two windows left and right of the television set, so if anything had happened I would have heard it, too,' Mr Bucket says.

Camelia reaffirms, 'So there was no more noise than any other days, and you didn't see anything strange last night?'

Mr. Bucket nodded in agreement. 'No, it was like any other night. Why are you asking, sweetheart?'

'Oh, we invited some friends over for a party, and the music was slightly louder than usual, so we thought we made a lot of noise. We hope we didn't disturb your evening.'

'Not at all; the night was serene. I remember I walked to the window to draw the curtain at midnight, and only felt the breeze of the air brushing my face, then realized I forgot to close the windows. I felt so peaceful, so I continued watching the stars and sky for a few minutes before shutting it. However, while I was gazing at the stars and sky, I overheard a car exhaust with a man's voice whispering. Other than that, I didn't hear or see anything peculiar close to your house.'

'Mr. Bucket, you said you heard a car and men's voices last night… Did you by any chance hear what they were saying or what they were looking at?' Camelia asks.

'Not that I can recall at the moment, but I will let you

know if I remember anything,' Mr. Bucket replies. 'What is your mother's name?' he asks.

'Casendra Miles,' Camelia replies.

He blinks as if confused. 'I can't recall if I've talked to her before. Anyway, run along, young ladies, I'm due for my nap, and if I don't take a nap, I will end up telling you rubbish. Please send my regards to Casendra,' Mr. Bucket says with a smile.

'Mr. Bucket, this is our telephone number if you happen to remember anything. Please don't hesitate to call us,' Louise says.

Once they leave Mr. Bucket's house, they turn to the right of Camelia's house to visit another neighbour. 'It seems unreal that in their eyes, nothing happened last night while we felt it was so real. Bizarre, right?' Camelia says to Louise.

Louise nods in agreement. Upon reaching the neighbour's house, it is surrounded with darkness as Louise peers through the window beside the entrance door.

'What are you looking at?' a lady snaps in their ear, which startles them both, and they turn their heads to face eye to eye with a baby blue eye, greyish brownish hair tie in a bun.

'Hi there, I'm your neighbour Camelia, and this is my friend Louise, we apologize for trespassing, we didn't mean to, we've wanted to say hi to you ever since I moved here a year ago. I haven't met you personally.' Camelia extended her hand to shake.

'Oh, that is kind of you, I am in a rush for a meeting with my family, but you can pop in next time?'

'We won't take long, just five to ten minutes of your time,

please?' Camelia asks politely.

'Alright, since you insisted. But I only have ten minutes. By the way, Camelia, you may call me Mrs. Daisy Lee.'

'We were just wondering; did we make a lot of noise yesterday evening? Any screaming, loud music, animals growling? We were afraid we must have made a lot of disturbance to the neighbours for our college get together party.'

'No, I remember well, the night was peaceful as usual, and I was having dinner with my husband, Mr. Lee, at our garden terrace, and we didn't hear anything except for the usual cricket. At midnight, we heard Mr. Bucket's dog barking, but it was a usual tone of barking, nothing unusual. Not to worry, Camelia and Louise, you didn't disturb us at all with your party. Have a nice day,' Mrs. Daisy says.

'Thanks, Mrs. Daisy.' The door slams in their faces before Camelia can finish her sentence.

'Unbelievable! Interesting Louise…the findings from my neighbours are the same. Nothing out of the ordinary…'..

CHAPTER 9

On Monday at the college, Camelia and Louise pass a lecture room. Its door is transparent. Louise stammers, 'Is that Jamie, Vanessa, Zoe, Alexia, and Tom? The supposedly missing and dead students from your house party last Friday.' They turn to look at the lecture class again via the transparent door, and abruptly stop to watch them laughing and throwing paper at each other. They are in one piece; they don't look injured and look completely fine. All five of them are laughing. 'Amazing, none of them are dead as per our experience; I wonder if they are real or we were under the influence of a hallucination,' Louise whispers to Camelia.

'I have an idea,' Camelia says.

Before she can say anything, she feels something poking her in her side. 'Ouch! Ouch! Stop it, Louise; what are you doing?'

'What? I'm not doing anything; what is it?' Louise asks,

clearly alarmed, while at the same time, she shows both her hands to Camelia that her hands aren't doing anything.

Camelia's bag pack handle is suddenly being pulled aside abruptly in a forceful manner, making her choke. Her face becomes pale while both of her hands are waving for help in the air, pulling and scrambling to release the bag-sling handle twisting her neck and body to the left.

'Why do you look pale?' Louise asks.

Alarmed, looking at Camelia's bag swaying forcefully downward while pulling Camelia's neck with it, quick as a flash, Louise takes a penknife from her backpack. Then, she places it on the sling handle to cut it loose and release Camelia from choking. Unfortunately, while she's cutting, someone knocks her shoulder hard, which causes her hand to let go of the penknife, which accidentally hits Camelia's chest, causing her to bleed.

'Oh my, what is happening? Sorry!' Louise cries. She picks up the penknife and, this time, cuts the handle, and finally, the bag's handle comes off, releasing it from Camelia's neck as her bag falls on the floor.

'Let's go to the sickbay,' Louise whispers to Camelia. She hugs her and leads her by her hand, and as they are both about to start walking, Zoe comes out from the lecture class.

'So, someone is in big trouble; I saw you trying to murder your friend with a penknife.'

'No! No! You got it all wrong. I tried to save her from choking; however, I accidentally dropped the penknife on her chest,' Louise defends herself.

Zoe grins wickedly and blows a bubble gum bubble in

Louise's face.

Within five minutes, Louise and Camelia make their way to the sick bay located opposite the cafeteria; they are unaware of Ms. Lai tailing them closely at the back.

'Hey, you two, Louise and Camelia, stop immediately!' Ms. Lai shouts. Ms. Lai the disciplinary administrator of the college in her forty's, with wrinkles on her forehead. She is fierce; therefore a majority of the students dare not play a fool.

Some students pass by and abruptly stop looking at Ms. Lai, then turn to look at Camelia and Louise, and upon seeing blood on Camelia's blouse, their eyes widen, and they run away as fast as they can.

Both abruptly stop with the instructions they hear from Ms. Lai. Camelia bleeds more at the chest, while Ms. Lai holds her hands to help her walk to the sick bay, which is five hundred metres away from where they're standing. Upon reaching the sick bay, the nurse in charge sees the blood penetrating Camelia's blouse and quickly assists Ms. Lai and Louise to place Camelia on the bed. 'What has happened?' the nurse asks, and Louise quickly explains what happened.

'I am so careless, I am so sorry,' Louise says between sobs.

'Now, now, this is not the time to cry,' Ms. Lai interrupts.

The nurse opens Camelia's blouse, takes the clean gauze that was placed in a vacuum plastic, cleans her wound with water and a sterile substance to remove debris and dirt.

'Ouch! Ouch!' Camelia exclaims in pain while gripping hard on the cloth spread out on the sickbay bed to withhold the stinging pain.

'The cut is quite deep and will require an X-ray as well as

an extensive examination. As the cut is near to the chest, a professional medical examiner is required to do the check-up.'

'Her mother is away during the weekdays, so I will accompany her to the hospital,' Louise says.

'No, I will accompany both of you, so nothing funny continues to happen. I am yet to question both of you regarding this incident, and to clear Louise of attempted murder,' Ms Lai says.

'What? I am not what you think Ms. Lai; we have known each other since childhood, we are best friends. How could I ever intentionally hurt her?' Louise says, her voice trembling.

After a thorough examination by the doctor, X-rays results are out within an hour, and to their relief, there is nothing serious. It's a cut at the surface of Camelia's chest, so no surgery is required. Instead, the doctor applies medication on the open wound as well as a bandage to prevent from any further complications and scarring. Within hours, Camelia is discharged, then in the same afternoon, all three of them return to the college to clear things out.

Ms. Lai brings them to the discipline office in college for questioning. Zoe is called in for questioning since she was the one who informed Ms. Lai of the incident. Ms. Lai and Assistant Discipline teacher Mr. Terry are present during the questioning. 'I have the evidence Ms. Lai; I have recorded all the sequence of events in my phone's camera,' Zoe says while holding her mobile mid-air to show her latest Samsung. 'Let me show you that Louise is the murderer!' Zoe raises her voice; then she starts playing the video, which manages to capture the event from the sling bag handle. 'She tries to strangle her best friend; look how she tries to pull the bag further down, which may cause abbreviation of a throat cut. Look! Look here, she pulls out the penknife from her bag pocket, then it hits Camelia's chest. This evidence is sufficient to charge Louise as a psychopath or an attempted murderer,' Zoe says in a shivering voice and wraps her arms around herself.

'Enough of the accusations, Zoe. We will put Louise under a watchful eye supervision program whereby she isn't to get close to Camelia for two solid weeks,' Ms. Lai says.

'But… But I need to accompany Camelia as she is staying alone on the weekdays,' Louise pleads.

'For now, Camelia can stay by herself in her own house since she is an adult and fit from the slight injury, and she has the accessibility to call me for any emergency,' Ms. Lai says.

She extends her hand, pulls Louise close to her harshly, and takes a clean medical tong, places a tiny detecting chip at the side of her ear; another detector chip is placed at the battery compartment of her black swatch wrist watch. I'll be monitoring you closely,' Ms. Lai says sternly to Louise.

'Can't I defend myself here?' Louise asks while looking down, picks up her bag pack, steals a peck on Camelia's cheek, and leaves the room by closing the door behind her.

***

Camelia rests at the sick bay until it closes.

'Up you go home now, would you like me to call a taxi for you?' the nurse politely asks.

She shakes her head and says, 'I will be alright.' The nurse extends her hand and gives Camelia a piece of paper. 'Here is my mobile number in case of any emergencies. Please call me immediately,' the nurse continues.

Camelia takes the paper, slips it into her pants pocket then takes her sling backpack. But since the handle is torn into two, the only way to carry them is by hugging them as she walks away.

Camelia walks out of the sick bay, still deep in her thoughts of the morning's incident. She walks without realising she is walking backwards instead of approaching the exit door to leave the college.

She's exhausted from the pain in her chest as well as her feelings since she momentarily lost her childhood friend due to a ridiculous accusation from Zoe. After ambling for a few minutes, she realises she is facing the wrong direction. Instantly she corrects herself by turning her face and body to turn the correct direction of the exit door. As she's about to turn and renew her direction, she sees the wording 'Security Department' signage hanging above a door at the end of the right side from where she is standing. 'I have to clear Louise's name,' Camelia says to herself. She walks toward the said department and knocks on the door. She stands for a minute; however, there is no response, so she extends her hand, twists the doorknob, and this time it feels light when she pushes the door harder.

'Yes, young girl, what are you doing here? Lectures are over,' one of the security personnel says.

'Hi, I'm Camelia. There was an incident this morning just outside the Physics lecture class. Can I see the full video footage?' Camelia asks.

'Oh my! Alright, when we saw the live footage we didn't considered it as an incident. We thought your friend was fooling around with you. You know, jokingly pulling the bag. We didn't concentrate the whole time. Please come in to share the details for us to investigate via the CCTV.'

'Hi, I am Berry, the most senior security personnel here. '

'My friend Louise has been wrongly penalised by Ms. Lai, so I'm searching for evidence,' Camelia says.

'Standard procedure once an incident is made known, the first thing that Ms. Lai often does is asking to view the video footage. Surprisingly, this time Ms. Lai didn't request for any video footage before making any judgements, and that's so unlike her,' Berry says while massaging the neat moustache just above his lips.

'Today's date: 27th August, the time of the incident is at ten in the morning, let me shift the timing on the mother board to nine. This is because we'd like to watch for the surroundings earlier, whether any culprit is hidden or looming around the college compound. You never know, they could be preparing anything at the incident grounds,' Berry explains as Lewis navigates the lever to rewind the video's live footage.

'Hmm, nothing peculiar here, Ms. Camelia. I'd appreciate your watchful eye as we rewind and replay the video footage,' Berry explains.

'Yes, of course,' Camelia says.

At 9.56:12 in the morning, a dark greyish maroon hood can be seen moving from one end to another end amongst the crowded students. It moves super-fast, but the figure is gone when the footage moves to 9.57 am. Where is it?

'Ok, so we are to watch out for this greyish maroon colour hood, and we need to identify if the person is one of our college students,' Berry says to Lewis. At ten in the morning, the greyish maroon hood looks like it's leaving the gents toilet, then enters the janitor's room.

'Lewis, can you shift the footage closer and zoom in so that we can identify anything peculiar about this person?'

'Let's look at the janitor's room; what time does this person leave?' At exactly 10.05 am, the door opened widely with a trolley with cleaning supplies just about to leave the room. Lewis magnifies the footage and sees…

'Oh, it's just Ali, our usual janitor,' exclaims Lewis. 'We are left with no suspicious characters.'

'Hmm, never mind. Louise and Camelia, please continue watching this footage, and I'm sure we will find something soon. While you and Louise watch the footage, let me call Ali to ensure he was the one who wore the hoodie this morning,' Berry continues. Berry takes out his radio. 'Ali, how have you been my man? Where are you? I would like to have a minute or two of your time, like right now.'

Berry leaves the room and walks across the hall to the janitor room, located two metres from the college entrance.

'Woah, that is fast, Berry, it is like lightning; I was in the midst of finalising my cleaning, just placing my trolley into the janitor's room.'

While Berry went to interview Ali, Camelia manages to sneak out and follow Berry to hear his conversation with Ali. 'Lewis, I think I left something at the sick bay. I will return after that to continue watching the CCTV footage.'

She was hiding beside the wall nearby the janitor. Camelia strains her ears to hear the conversation: 'Did you see anything fishy going on around the college this morning? Did you see anyone that isn't the college students hanging around the college?' Berry asks while Ali is busy parking his cleaners' trolley inside the room. Ali takes his greyish maroon hood from the wall hanger before pulling it on.

'Nope, this place looks normal, just that I heard there was an incident nearby at one of the lecture classes, there was a student strangled by her friend,' says Ali. 'I think there's another student who played a prank on her and her friend. You'd better check it out, this college is getting creepier ever since the management was bought over by a bunch of wealthy billionaires... can't recall his name,' Ali continues in a whisper. 'Must be bad money laundering somewhere.' Ali chuckles.

After hearing this conversation, Camelia creeps back to the Security Department to resume the footage search.

***

'Wait...pause!' Camelia shouts excitedly at Lewis. 'Please rewind by a few seconds. Stop right now, did you see there was a long arm pulling my sling bag pack handle? Did you see the skinny hands jolting out from the height of my waist?'

'Oh my, the person's height is very short for an ordinary person. Can it be an Asian person's height?' Camelia asks.

Lewis shrugs off and says, 'I really don't know how to make out the person trying to choke you.'

'Please save a copy of this footage in order to clear my

friend's name from defamation. I am relieved that I can find a piece of evidence on the attacker; at least we are aware that there is someone else who tries to strangle me.'

'Woah, wait, see that!' Lewis exclaims. 'The thief is wearing a Halloween mask to cover their identity,' Lewis continues. 'I'm recording this for the disciplinary hearing and for us to report to the police; this is serious,' adds Lewis.

'Berry, we saw the thief; however, it wore a mask; we are to investigate this and tighten the college's security,' says Lewis via the radio.

'Stop it...rewind by a few seconds...stop right there!' Camelia shouts excitedly. 'Please magnify the footage, especially his or her hand...the exact symbol as the ones I saw somewhere... it's like a part of the missing diamond shape!'

'Woah, you meant you have seen the symbol before …...is it in this college? Camelia, if you and your friend are investigating the incident that happened to Lucas, Henry, and Professor Edwin, I would advise you against it. This is a dangerous criminal activity.'

'Don't get me wrong Lewis, Louise and I are not investigating this case or any cases, just that I thought I saw it elsewhere which I cannot recall at the moment,' Camelia replies.

***

'Hello Louise, you know what? I have good news for you....you are free from the defamation; we saw a culprit via the college video footage,' says Camelia via her phone.

'What? See, I told you I'm innocent!' Louise says.

'We will meet tomorrow in college, and let's meet with the Principle John, Ms. Lai, for her carelessness of not handling this case prudently, and make sure she will discharge you accordingly,' Camelia says with a smile.

'Yes, we should meet with the Principle to clear my name once and for all.'

***

The next day in the principal's John office, Ms. Lai, Terry, Assistant Discipline Teacher, Zoe, Berry, and Lewis from the security department are called upon for a discussion. 'Ms Lai, from today onward, you aren't to charge any students without any concrete evidence from our security team. We cannot rely on another student video since it was from another angle that doesn't show the reality,' Principal John says. 'Terry, please ensure all cases arrange for a proper hearing before any punishment is implemented on students.'

'Yes, sir,' Mr. Terry replies.

With that, Ms. Lai takes out a clean tong and a small blade to remove the chip beside Louise's ear and takes off Louise's wrist watch to remove the chip hidden in the battery compartment. 'I apologize for wrongly accusing you, Louise; I will be extra careful next time,' Ms. Lai says.

'Another thing, Terry, please write a report for closure of this incident for the accusation against Ms. Louise. Then he turns his head facing the security team; Lewis and Berry, you are both required to do an open investigation and tighten the college campus since the safety of our students and staff is of the greatest importance.'

Principal John says. 'All are adjourned, thanks, and take care,' he continues. During the discussion, Zoe remains quiet, looking small, slouching as though she is trying to hide amongst the crowd. Suddenly her face turns cheerful when the principal dismisses the discussion.

'Excuse me, Principle John, I would suggest that since Zoe gave the video evidence to Ms. Lai, swayed as well as convinced Ms. Lai on the so called accusation, I would suggest an appropriate punishment should be given to her as a lesson,' Camelia says.

'Hold on, everyone. Camelia, thanks for bringing up this issue. I have overlooked Zoe's behaviour in this matter. Zoe will be fined as well and she will undergo community service immediately for six months. I'm appointing Terry lead in ensuring Zoe adheres to this punishment.'

Once the discussion is dismissed, the Security Department personnel continue their investigation.

Berry says, 'Excuse me, Camelia and Louise, I need to retain you for our further investigation, please follow us to the Security Department.'

Camelia and Louise nod in agreement. *Unbelievable, the investigation should have been initiated earlier; the day itself of the incident for clues/traces*, Camelia says under her breath.

'We'd like to check the sling bag that caused the choking

for any fingerprints. After that, we will be sending your bag to the police station for identification. Also, do you have anyone in or outside school that might be holding a grudge against both of you?'

'Not that I know of; we are often together,' Camelia replies. 'The other classmates we are not close, but we just mingle during lectures. There is jealousy amongst five people, mostly on my grades. However, they are harmless as they only put a small prank and make fun of me in lectures.'

'We don't mix or go for parties with other college students,' Louise adds. 'Look at that cut on your neck,' Lewis exclaims as he sees it whilst Camelia is adjusting her top collar. 'There is an additional cut other than the choking mark. Please take a look in this mirror.'

Camelia stands up and walks to the hanging mirror that is placed on top of a shelf. 'Hmm, interesting.' Camelia takes a selfie and starts touching it. *I didn't notice this earlier; has it just appeared?* It feels rough with a shape; it isn't a deep wound, however, it looks like a symbol. 'If I were to put the puzzle pieces together, it looks like one petal of four small pieces of a diamond shape,' Camelia whispers to Louise.

Louise takes out her phone and snaps a photo of it as evidence, which she sends it to Berry for their investigation and Camelia for their very own investigation.' Does the symbol mean I have any correlation with Lucas? What about the leather book on Mum's table? Does this mean I will be the next victim, or will I be the one to save Lucas? I feel uncomfortable and have to be on alert of my whereabouts,' Camelia says to Louise while frowning.

Louise's forehead puckered, and her brows pulled together. 'I am worried for your safety, Cam. How can I protect you from these strange happenings? Sigh.'

CHAPTER 10

They knock at the door, but there is no response. 'This must be the correct address as indicated in the discipline department book attendance, I snapped.' They try again. Eventually, the door opens slightly.

'Hi, I'm Zoe's college friend; we are dropping over to say hi to her,' Camelia says.

'Zoe! Zoe! Your college friends are here,' shouts Zoe's mother. She is petite with a mole visible on her left chin, looks in her thirties, wearing a pair of glasses. She appears pleasant at first sight.

'Oh, it's you, what do you want?' Zoe asks in an irritated tone. Her face turns hostile with her lips curled up. She is leaning against the ajar door, with her hands crossed over her chest.

'We'd like to ask you a few things for confirmation if you don't mind,' Camelia says.

'Just make it quick,' Zoe replies sternly.

'Last Saturday, we saw you in Camelia's house when we played 'Wink murderer' at her house's get-together party. Did you experience anything strange?' Louise asks.

Zoe's eyes widen with bewilderment. 'Woah, wait, why should I be at Camelia's house for a party when I was at Jamie and Alexia's birthday party bash? Jamie's house is so huge; it's a $25,000,000 mansion with a swimming pool and gym. I definitely chose to go to his house rather than yours. I'd better go in; I have lots of things to do,' Zoe replies bluntly.

Camelia and Louise glance at each other. 'You, Jamie, Vanessa, Tom, and Alexia came along for games and drinking at my house last Saturday…remember?' Camelia says while looking at Zoe's eyes to determine if she is lying. But her stare and eyes tell them nothing.

Zoe's eyes open wide when Camelia mentions those names. 'All of them were with me at Jamie's party. 'Get your hands off me! I will never go to a party at yours… you're so nerdy,' Zoe replies arrogantly before closing the door in their faces.

'So your party didn't materialise, but we felt the creature was real, we found its fur on the ground, but all others seem to be intact. This doesn't make any sense,' Louise says. 'Let's visit Professor Carlos and discuss with him.'

***

They hear a low, growling noise. 'What was that? Louise asks. They're walking toward Professor Carlos's house after having a quick dinner at Subway. They turn their heads and catch sight of a huge shadow following them within the trees. 'Come, let's quicken our steps; we are a hundred feet away from his house according to the google route map,' Camelia says. They're both panting with sweaty palms. Camelia falls splat on the grass since she's trembling in fear. Within fifteen minutes, they see Professor Carlos's entrance veranda a hundred metres from their location. 'We are nearing,' Camelia says; she grabs hold of Louise's hand, hoping she will walk faster.

Unexpectedly, the sound resonates as they're about to twist the doorknob. 'Oh my god!' There is no light in this veranda; it's in pitch darkness. 'Wait, let me get the house keys from my jacket pocket.'

'Take out the key quick,' Louise exclaims in a panicked voice.

'I am, but I can't feel them. Can you flash the light into my pocket?' Camelia says. Hastily, Louise takes out her mobile torch and shines it. 'It isn't in this pocket. I need to unzip the centre. I see it!'

'Got it!' Camelia says.

She places the key into the keyhole; however, it doesn't fit. 'No! No! No! It's the wrong key; it must be my house key,' Camelia exclaims. 'Maybe it's at the other side of the pocket; I must grab it fast.' Hurriedly, with the help of the small light from a torch, Louise is holding, Camelia manages to take out the rusty golden key. As she's about to place the key into the hole, her trembling hand releases it, and it crashes onto the veranda floor. 'Oh no!' she cries.

Louise bends down to pick up the key then places it into

the keyhole. She twists the doorknob. With heavy breathing, both run into the house at top speed, hitting each other while doing it, then Camelia close and lock the door behind them just in time as they hear and see the shadows of creatures and hear the growling sound.

'Ouch!' A thick writing pad hits Louise on the forehead at the entrance hallway. Camelia is beyond belief upon seeing this.

Then words written on the pad become visible, 'You two ladies, please follow me to my laboratory location in my basement, just follow the green glow on the dark wrist band.'

'Are you Professor Carlos?' Louise asks, rubbing her forehead.

'Yes, it's me.'

'Phew! So many events have happened in order to gather all the specimens,' Camelia continues.

They walk closely together by referring to the glow wrist band, knocking on some furniture as they pass since they're unable to gauge the furniture's diameter as the house is in pitch darkness. 'Let me put on the house light and see where the switch is,' Louise says. The house is bright.

'No lights for safety!' writes the Professor. However, it's too late because the creatures outside clearly saw the lights because they begin to scamper around and start making a lot of noise on the Professor's roof.

The high-pitched sounds can be heard from above their heads. Suddenly, goosebumps appear on Camelia's both hands. They stare at each other with worried eyes. Realising the lights have activated the amok of the creature outside,

Louise instantly shuts off the lights and the noise dies down slowly; the creatures disappear as the house becomes still. Camelia signals at Louise to keep quiet and resume following Professor Carlos's lead.

They walk across the living room, then pass a kitchen in dark green background before entering another white tiled kitchen with rundown walls. Finally, the glowing band turns to the left, opening a door that has a room for pantry storage, and they push a hidden white button situated at the back of the shelf containing a variety of cereals.

'Move aside!' the Professor writes on the pad.

They jump aside as the floor located near to the cupboard trembles, and an opening appears below their feet. 'Please pull the lever up,' writes the Professor. Camelia gives it a nudge, and the door opens. Automatically, a wooden staircase with very few steps is visible.

'Please follow me,' Professor Carlos writes. All three of them start to climb down the steps, and the Professor reverts by climbing the stairs again, pulls the lever down, and the door automatically closes behind them. Then, automatically, the lights turn on brightly. 'Now, you may speak in a normal tone,' the Professor writes.

'Finally! What a horrible experience,' Louise says. It was scary and puzzling, but Camelia is relieved they can finally breathe normally and releases a sigh.

'This place is cool – there is a complete test laboratory with equipment, beakers, burners, and other tools necessary to complete experiments,' Louise says as she walks around the place.

'By the way, do you remember your conclusion about your ability to see me during the night with the torch? Well, see for yourself...it isn't working as the days goes by,' the Professor says.

Camelia takes out the broken pieces of the bee-like glass on the lab's steel table, a creature's fur laid out on a small plate covered with a clean tissue, and two small cotton swab boxes containing her mother's saliva and a strand of her hair. With the look of the items, the Professor becomes excited and instantly switches on the Nexus microscope, then takes the fur from the plate with a clean tong onto the Bunsen.

In order to obtain the outcome of any specimen study, they must observe any strange phenomena when it arises. This encompasses identifying different types of species; clarifying them into categories that are relevant to them. Once identifying and defining is done, next is to map the result with the existing data for observation and examine its characteristics. From there, we can make a conclusion whether the specimen is from animal, human being or others,' Louise explains.

'There goes the top student talking on her favourite subject,' Camelia says, winking at Louise. Correct me if I am wrong in my understanding of your recent explanation, Louise; you are saying that a scientist will observe for any strange outcome after mixing the appropriate chemicals into the items we found?

From the study, scientists will then identify and categorize accordingly whether the test or items we found is from animal or human being or anything else.'

'Spot on.' Louise replies.

'If the research and analysis via Biology and chemicals don't provide profound results, the data analytics scientist will be the next to do the research. Which encompasses; identifying the origins and substances of the creature; as we all know with advanced technology how the artifacts or processes were created or mutated to satisfy the hunger of human needs,' Camelia adds.

'Very intellectual indeed,' the Professor writes.

'Let's begin the experiment.'

Louise mixed a chemical into a Bunsen; then she placed the creatures' fur onto a small plate; once mixed immediately, a result churned out. 'According to the test results we've mixed with chemicals, the fur is made of a few thousand molecules and electrons,' Louise says. As she reads the results after the Professor mixes them with another investigation chemicals. 'Hmm... interesting findings…Never before seen in any animals before,' Louise utters. 'Let's mix the fur with another type of chemical; maybe it matches.' Professor writes. Then Professor pours a greenish liquid mixed with the fur.. the result is that it is a mixture of reptiles and furry animals. Louise talks out loudly.

'That is correct, interesting findings,' the Professor interrupts while he writes his response on a writing pad, then Camelia and Louise sees his hankie moving upwards; the hankie looks slightly wet afterwards folded and kept in his pocket. Meanwhile, let me keep this item lock in the coding refrigerator, and we are to continue research on other elements like your mother's saliva and hair,' the Professor writes.

'While you are at it, Professor and Louise, let me try my expertise to reverse the invisible Professor; maybe there is an explanation in data analytics division the development of an invisible substance,' Camelia says, smiles and high fives Louise. 'Professor, keep still; I will need a specimen to do this experiment.' Camelia takes out a scarp and tong and extends her hand in mid-air; near to Professor's glowing wrist band, she instantly places it in a bottle, which she puts into the radiation box for testing. Then another sample is taken and placed into a bottle.

'Let me develop the time machine travel in order to do the testing on another sample of the Professor; I have a hunch a time traveller zapped him,' says Camelia, casting Louise a wink.

Camelia, in her thoughts, with the diamond symbol that Henry and herself have, feels there is a connection between Professor Carlos being invisible and the ten students and that it must all be related to a wacko scientist's invention. Maybe the Professor was a failure or a prototype.

Soon, they would find out the truth.

***

After midnight, Camelia and Louise reach Camelia's home safely. When they turn the doorknob, the sound of rusty leaves and tree branches can be heard from upstairs, and both turn to look at each other. Camelia signals to Louise to keep quiet, and Camelia says she will go to the side to get the ladder to climb up via the side of the lower level roof. Louise nods in an agreement, as well as signalling that she will take the shovel that is placed at the side of the big vase of lilies.

With the dim torchlight in her mouth, Camelia climbs the ladder slowly in order not to make any sound. When she makes it to the lower level of her house rooftop on the same level as her bedroom, she freezes as if she's seen a ghost, surprised to find her window open wide with lots of dried leaves covering the floor. 'What a mess; how are we going to sleep here tonight?' Camelia mutters under her breath. As she's about to backtrack her steps, since no intruder can be identified, suddenly a shadow catches her eye. It appears to be a huge man or creature, but she can't figure it out as it's approximately eight feet tall with a muscular build. When she sees this, Camelia quickly grabs her mobile from her jeans pocket, presses favourite and dials Louise.

Unexpectedly, a loud thud can be heard in the quiet surroundings of the house. Louise turns to face the noise and witnesses three shadows, all three of them of the same overbearing height running at top speed, away from the house. Camelia climbs down the ladder, immediately switches on the veranda lights, opens her house door, enters then turns on the garden terrace lights to ensure no intruders around the compound. After being frozen upon seeing the three shadows, Louise enters in haste, fearing the three shadow intruders might reappear. 'I will activate the alarm once all doors and windows are closed; let me go upstairs to close my window,' Camelia says to Louise.

'Let me follow you!' Louise exclaims in fear.

Once they reach the upstairs floor, Camelia activates

the pathway lights. Louise, still holding a shovel in her right hand, stands beside Camelia's bedroom door panel to be on guard for any anomalies. At the same time, Camelia manages to get hold of a 'chef's knife' (one of many types of kitchen knives) kept in the kitchen drawer before walking upstairs, planning to stab the intruder in the head if they were to attack. Camelia slightly lifts the door to prevent any creaking sound, then swings it quickly in a single motion. 'Phew! She activates the lights, and, to their surprise, her bedroom is clean, with none of the dirty leaves she saw scattered in her room a few minutes ago via the rooftop.

'Anybody here?' Louise shouts bravely. However, there is no response, and Camelia walks further, step by step, into her room, toward the window direction to close and lock it. Then Louise checks underneath her bed, bathroom, cupboard, and writing table; however, it's unperturbed.

'Guess the coast is clear, and we're safe,' Louise continues.

That night, they both sleep like a log, exhausted from all of the chasing and running.

At five in the morning, a wooden drum can be heard coming from Camelia's mother's bedroom. 'Louise, stop it!' says Camelia. 'So noisy. Erm… shut up!' A few minutes later, the sound repeats itself, this time louder. She is startled by the noise, opens her eyes, skimming her view of the whole room on her side of the bed. 'Louise, won't you shut up?' Camelia shouts again. Then she turns to face Louise, slaps her mouth as she falls fast asleep again.

'What?' Louise responds in a sleepy voice, then continues sleeping. The drum sounds increasingly loudly in Camelia's ears. Therefore, it's too noisy for her to sleep. The sound lingers, and she tightens her lips while starting to fold both of her hands to withhold her anger of being disturbed while she's so sleepy.

This time the sound isn't only loud but beats quickly, forcing her awake. She blinks, then whispers in Louise's ear, 'I'm going to look in Mum's bedroom; it's too noisy here.'

Louise takes another pillow from beside her and covers her ears.

Camelia gets up from her bed, takes her dark blue woollen sweater hanging beside her mirror table, quietly pulls open the middle drawer of her mirror table, and takes out the chef's knife she keeps for safety.

Then she confidently walks toward the door, opens it slightly, peeping through it, ensuring there is no intruder at large, and opens it fuller.

Suddenly the sound stops, and the house is silent.

'Guess it was in my dreams,' Camelia says to herself, yawns and retraces her steps, then turns her face and body to re-enter her room before closing the door behind her, then walks to her bed, pulls the comforter over herself as her eyes are about to close.

The drumming sounds resurgence, forcing Camelia's eyes to open widely. 'Unbelievable.' She takes her pillow, folds them into two, and covers her ears. 'That's better,' she says.

The thudding sounds louder than usual as she dozes off and repetitively. 'Argh! This noise is making me go crazy!' she says, at the same time pushing her comforter harshly aside as she's impatient to stop the noise. She gets up, takes the knife for protection, and opens the door. This time she does it faster since she feels irritated by the noise and is adamantly wanting to put it to a stop.

She leaves her room quickly, closing her bedroom door behind her for Louise's safety. As she shuts the door, sudden adrenaline caused by fear creeps into her heart, and she tries to retract by twisting her room knob, but it's locked inside. She shakes it with her fist, but it doesn't budge open. 'Well, let me face it by myself; I can do it!' Camelia whispers to herself. Initially, she tiptoes, then feeling tired from it, she starts walking cautiously, inch by inch, closer to the source of the noise and passes the window with a small table on the way to her mother's bedroom. Next, Camelia checks the window, but it's completely shut. Then she draws the curtain aside to peep outside however, it's pitch black with street lights.

There are no vehicles nor people wandering around her neighbourhood. The house sounds silent as she peeps through the window. Then, the loud noise suddenly dies.

'Well, I must be dreaming,' she tells herself. She begins to turn and walk away when suddenly her heart beats faster and faster, sweat trickles down her neck, and she can hear some whispering coming from her mother's room. Her hands begin to tremble with fear. She breathes deeply to give her confidence.

The wooden drum sounds again as though inviting Camelia to join whatever event the intruder or scientist is organising. Camelia quickens her steps as she's eager to find out what it is after a few months of repeatedly hearing this sound.

When she reaches the destination; feeling brave; Camelia springs open the door with the chef's knife in mid-air, getting ready to stab her attacker, when to her surprise, a firm hand closes over her nose and mouth. Camelia struggles and kicks her leg onto the intruder's belly, however to no avail.

Within split seconds, she's incapacitated. The intruder ties her to and blindfolds her with a piece of black cloth. Within an hour or so, Camelia is invigorated from the chloroform inhaler; as she tries opening her eyes, she feels her eyes are tightly bound. It's pitch black, and both of her hands are tightly tied behind her back. 'Where am I? What do you want?' Camelia tries to shout, but her voice sounds muffled within the bandage that gagged her. Then she keeps quiet, trying to figure out any sound she recognises; but the place is silent. Subsequently, Camelia tries to wake up from the mattress, however, her two feet are bound with thick rope. Within a few minutes, a ray of light seeps into her bindings, and she hears three footsteps approaching; she feels a skinny hand touching hers; then they start to unbutton Camelia's pyjamas. She starts screaming and shaking in fear of being raped.

Consequently, a firm hand she recognises from earlier holds both of her arms tightly as the hand button down her completely. 'You idiot, this is not the 'one', there is no symbol,' they shout harshly. Immediately, two strong hands place the new chloroform onto Camelia's nose, and she falls unconscious.

Eventually, after a few hours, she opens her eyes to stare up at a ceiling...her room. 'Oh my!' Her head is dizzy; her ceiling looks round like a merry-go-round. Camelia lays back against a pillow to ensure the stability of her head. Within ten minutes, she tries to tilt her head to the left but feels dizzy, and she starts to wake up from the bed slowly. Suddenly Camelia remembers the whole event, which flashes in her mind like a dream. She thinks back on the smell that made her dizzy and unconscious; the skinny fingers fondled her belly button then went to the left and right side of her waist and just under her breast, remembering how it all felt so real.

She got up abruptly thinking about this and walks straight to the mirror in the bathroom; her top pyjamas are in the tag, it's untouchable, and her buttons are neatly closed.

'Let me double-check.' Camelia undoes her top pyjamas button to find any evidence of any harassment done on her top. But there is nothing peculiar, so Camelia smiles at herself in the mirror. 'It was a weird dream after all.'

The next day Camelia reiterates her dream to Louise during breakfast. Maybe there is something fishy going on in Mum's room, and we must find out what it is, she thinks.

CHAPTER II

'Hello, I'm leading many back-to-back meetings and tight deadline projects,' her mother says over the phone.

'But Mum, it's my birthday, and you promised you'd be back,' Camelia replies sadly. 'Tell me your address, I can see you, and we will have a quick meal; I promise I won't be a nuisance.'

'No…No.. Don't you dare come here,' her mother's tone changes to one of anguish and fear. 'Er, what I meant was I won't have any time, and you'll be disappointed, go and buy something nice and spend time with Louise, just charge on my visa, I will WhatsApp you the number along with its pin.'

'Happy birthday, my darling Cam. I love you, but I urgently need to hang up now.'

'Well, happy birthday to me, I guess.' Camelia sighs with frustration. What is so great about her promotion and work that she doesn't have time for me? It's just for one day.

Then she hears her front doorknob twist before the door springs open, and Louise enters with a balloon in hand. 'Happy birthday! Why do you look so down and grumpy?' she asks. 'Your mother called me to say I will be the birthday organiser for the day!' Louise says and smiles.

With that sight, Camelia giggles.

'I love organising birthdays…so you will be my first victim.' Louise giggles. 'Are you ready? Close your eyes.' She places a light blue soft velvet cloth over Camelia's eyes and ties a knot at the back of her head. 'Hold my hands; we are going somewhere this morning,' Louise says.

'I'm excited,' Camelia says.

She passes the house hallway, then walks through the door. They pause momentarily while Louise locks the entrance door.

'Let me guess; we're at the Movenwater Spree?' Camelia asks.

Louise unties the knot, and the blindfolded is released. Camelia blinks twice to adjust her sight. She can see the jumping Waterloo area where toddlers play in the water. This is the entrance to the enormous water park.

'Oh my god. I love it. You are indeed the number one party organizer,' Camelia screams excitedly while hugging Louise with one of her legs up. 'Wait a minute, I didn't bring my swimming costume, so I cannot play on the rides,' Camelia shouts.

'Here…I snuck your swimming stuff in the bag, along with your goggles,' Louise says whilst she takes out Camelia's gear and watches Camelia smile.

'That is great!' Camelia exclaims.

Camelia and Louise walk and skip toward the entrance, singing happy birthday, and you are my sunshine as they go.

Camelia's mouth moves upwards, smiling at this thought as she likes adventurous rides like rollercoasters and swimming. However, this will be her first time combining roller coaster rides with water since Casendra is overprotective and has never agreed for her to participate in any so-called dangerous activities before.

In the spot they are standing in, they raise their heads to see the overview of the snake trail. 'Oh my God, it is long and colourful.'

'Yup, according to the information, the trail ride is as high as one hundred feet, six hundred foot long with mix colour of the bright yellow and orange slide.'

'No wonder it's named 'Snake Trail' because of its narrowness of the spaces and the long winding route,' Louise adds.

'Be my guest…The birthday girl will go first,' Louise says whilst chuckling at Camelia. 'We will meet each other at the end of the trail exit. Don't leave without me,' Louise adds swiftly since it is their turn and they need to move fast with the long queue.

Camelia sits down at the top edge of the trail ride, and emotion starts developing like fireworks exploding in her heart as she lays down with her head touching the fast-flowing water. Still, at least she tied her hair back in a ponytail so it wouldn't be a hindrance during the ride. 'One, two, three, four, five. Go! Enjoy!' Louise shouts while pushing her.

As Camelia leaves the entrance trail, Louise follows her. The route is long, fast, and winding, and there are lots of twists and turns that make the ride a blast. Camelia shuts her eyes, feeling slightly dizzy since it's her first experience.

However, as her body glides further down, she feels lighter in her heart and grins while raising her arms high up into the sky, waving excitedly and screaming her head off. She senses all her problems in the world she is shouldering have temporarily disappeared.

While she's dreaming about the serenity of the ride, she suddenly hears the screaming. It must be Louise following me, Camelia thinks, and smiles in satisfaction.

Water splashes on her face when she passes by, the feeling of freedom and joy spreading in her heart. Then, having a sharp hearing, she can hear the screams of laughter coming from the other side of the slide, and turns her head, facing another ride, smiles and tells herself she will ride the next one after this because it looks fun.

Unexpectedly, her giddiness resuscitates, and she quickly adjusts her head to the centre as per when she started; her head remains still as she doesn't dare move a muscle in case the movement aggravates her giddiness. She breathes in to stay calm and closes her eyes. As she glides further down but still at high height, she tries to raise her arms again, feeling the strong wind. Suddenly, the trail twists to the left, beneath a huge palm tree, and her buttocks slightly hit the slide on its side, which causes her to jolt, and she immediately opens her eyes widely, raises her head slightly to the side to check out, then feels satisfied it's part of the slide route and readjusts to strengthen her head.

A few minutes away from the corner of the shady leaves and trees, she raises her arms higher to feel the cool breeze of air.

Within a few seconds… 'Ouch!' Camelia exclaims, abruptly opens her eyes widely to see what is that's fallen on her hands. It's pretty heavy. Her heartbeat rises, and her hands start shaking when she feels exasperation. 'What is it that I just touched? Is it a dead bird?' Camelia says.

A loud shrieking sound comes from the other ride, leaving Camelia breathless. She starts to turn her head, tries to stop the ride, but she fears she may slip and hit something while she does that since the winding slide is full of fast-flowing water.

'What should I do?' Camelia says to herself.

Suddenly, she sees eye to eye with a guy with no shirt wearing orange Bermuda's, face looking pale, then sees one of his muscular, tanned arms stretching over the edge of the slide.

'Oh my! Is the slide broken?' Camelia says.

He is trying to push his heavyweight up the slide to save his life. He huffs and puffs as he tries to reach another side of the slide; however the fast, strong water current causes his hands to slip, bit by bit. 'Help! Help!' he shouts. 'Argh!' he adds, sounding panicked.

'Oh no! I hope he falls on the safety net. Is there one? I don't seem to recall seeing any, though,' Camelia says. Then, abruptly, her heart starts to feel like it might beat out of her chest. Her leg trembles as her arms grow tense. She closes her eyes momentarily, and once she opens them again, tears roll down from her cheek as she feels sorry for the guy.

A few minutes later, while she continues spiralling down from the ride, she is halfway through the ride, estimated three hundred feet high up the slide, when she feels it shudder abruptly. Then unexpected waves suddenly enter Camelia's nostrils which causes her to choke. She spews the water from her mouth and carries her head upward slightly to prevent more water from entering her nostrils. The slide changes its course as it moves further down to represent the snake tail of sharp curves. Initially, Camelia feels cold and short of breath, with butterflies in her stomach, but then the ride is smooth, and she sighs in relief. A few minutes later, she goes to some bend which makes her feel like she is going over the edge, and suddenly the feeling of nauseous, then waves of water come in to push her to move forward.

In a split second, a frightening shrieking voice can be heard from the slide. 'Oh no!' Camelia whispers to herself. Suddenly, as she curves to the right bend, she can see that the slide has given way a hundred metres below her feet. It falls to the ground with a crash and a metal pole that withstands the pillar of the slide drops, which causes the slides to fall apart one by one. Horror envelops Camelia's heart; she turns to check on Louise.

The rattling sound of a screw being loose can be heard loudly. She turns her head to see whether there is anything she can hold onto, preventing her from sliding further. Fortunately, the spot she is located is under a tree with branches. Camelia crouches down, and her right hand manages to grip the side of the slide. With the water flowing, it isn't easy to keep still on the side of the slide. Urgh…she jumps up from her spot, and her body is shaking with fear. She jumps and extends her arms to reach a branch above her head.

Luckily Louise comes sliding from above. She jumps off from her side, instantly grabbing Camelia's arms, huffs and puffs to give her a nudge, and pulls her. This leads Camelia to jump higher until she's finally able to hold the branch. Louise holds onto a metal pole beside the tree. Camelia swings her body to the bushes; however, in the midst of swinging, her grip is slippery, and she loses her balance and falls onto the broken slide.

'Help, help!' On the other hand, Louise manages to swing her body, leading her to land safely on the messy bushes with high grass. Upon witnessing Camelia falling, Louise's eyes and mouth open widely, shivering out of fear of her friends' fate and coldness from the water slide.

The water current becomes more potent on the slide.

Astounded by the sound, her heart beats faster, and sweat starts trickling down her neck, thinking of an alternative to save herself from falling to her death.

The other people appear, looking pale as ghosts, and some start gripping the side of the slide under the tree branches. Then, all ten of them hold hands, making a chain to ensure one by one jumps off onto the tree branches.

Louise, at the bushes, finds a SOS booth beside the tree and quickly dial for help.

Within a few minutes, a rescue helicopter flies by from afar; the rescue team sees Camelia gripping hard onto the edge of the slide board, trying her best not to fall. Her hands are covered with scratches and bleeding slightly.

The rescue team uses a megaphone. 'Lady, grab hold of the cable once we throw the rope with the end of the wire of the winch cable toward you.'

Camelia looks up, huffs, and puffs with her muscles tightening in her arms and legs, extending her right hand while her left grabs firmly onto the unstable slide to reach for the cable. She wriggles her body to stand halfway and stretches her arms out further. 'Come on, I must grab the cable this time. This is my last chance.' Fortunately, she manages to grab hold of the winch cable. The rescue team feels the nudge, tries to pull her inch by inch. Finally, Camelia's body and her legs are pulled up and roll over slowly onto the helicopter. Then the rescue team covers her with a thick towel in orange and belts her into her seat for safety.

Then they drive backward to save the other ten riders. Unfortunately, due to limited capacity, a helicopter can fit in only three pax, another rescue helicopter that is queuing for its turn in the back of this helicopter.

In the nick of time, all rescue timely; the last person out of the ten people had a narrow escape; the tree branch cracked… nearly broke into two when she managed to swing herself to catch the winch cable with her bare hands. The rescue team had to pull and roll the cable up to ensure she is safely in the helicopter before they can start flying. Upon entering the helicopter, the lady appears pale and frozen cold.

As the helicopter lands at the Movenparkwaves water park large parking space ample for the rescue helicopter to land, five ambulances appear at the water park entrance with paramedics and emergency doctors rushing out to help the rescue team to place the injured people on the stretchers.

One by one, ambulances drive off to the nearest hospital. The sight at the parking space of the water park is dreadful and pitiful for Camelia as she sees the faces of people incur cuts, and some require bandages on their heads and arms.

There are some who were unlucky to fall from a high height and had to endure fractured legs and hands crushes. She hears them groaning in pain. Due to the injury, the parking space turns temporary for injured people to rest while waiting for the ambulances to arrive.

When Camelia reaches the parking lot via the helicopter, a paramedic takes her to one of the ambulances to check her injuries. After seeing her injury is only slight cuts and bruises, they apply medicated lotion and bandages her legs and arms. Her eyes wander here and there while sitting at the exit of the ambulance door, searching for Louise. Once the paramedic settles her, she wanders around the parking lot, limping while she walks.

People who didn't ride the slides cry, taking the hands of their friends or families. Some look worried with stress wrinkles drawn on their foreheads.

She walks further, then stops temporarily close to a reporter doing live coverage on the incident. She hears the broadcast. 'Only one death from the Snake Trail was reported; the man was the first to fall from the Snake Trail when the bolt and slide gave way. It continues, the Black hurricane slide ride incident has unfortunately taken five lives. The slides all seem to be faulty at the same time. Most people who face cuts and bruises will be sent to hospital for treatment. Management has been called, and a further investigation will be conducted for any foul play or carelessness of the facilities department.'

Camelia turns her head to face the entrance and sees Louise's silhouette, turns her head again in the same direction. 'Louise! Louise!' Camelia shouts while limping, trying to walk faster to get hold of Louise, with her leg injured. She reduces her speed and groans in pain. She grimaces, trying to withhold the pain. This is so painful for me to catch up with Louise, but I'm glad she is safe.

CHAPTER 12

'Professor Carlos! Professor Carlos! Where are you?' Louise shouts.

They enter his house and are surprised that it appears peaceful from the hallway, living room, and kitchen.

'Woah. Someone must have spilled something... It smells gross,' Camelia says while opening the kitchen window since she can hardly breathe.

'It's a chemical smell and not any rotten food, I recognise this smell from the laboratory; you should put this over your nose as a precaution,' Louise says.

They walk toward another older kitchen where the odour is the strongest. They start coughing more while their faces turn red.

Camelia quickly opens all the windows and doors to prevent them from fainting.

Louise notices a cabinet made of steel beside the wash basin. It indicates chemical investigation materials.

Without wasting any time, she pulls the handle open, however it doesn't budge. She shakes it again and impatiently kicks the door. The handle comes off. The cabinet door opens, and to her relief, there are masks. She takes the face piece respiratory gas mask, wears it, and assists Camelia in putting hers on.

Camelia signals that she will go out to make a call for help 911 while Louise continues searching for Professor Carlos.

Louise starts walking further into a pantry storage room, eyes skimming for a glowing band that represents Professor Carlos. She clicks her torch and sees a glowing band on the floor, smacks it on his head when suddenly a pen slowly writes on a small pad, 'Help me, I'm suffocating. Hydrogen Sulfide.'

Ambulances, as well as the gas expert department, arrives after Camelia calls.

Two of the gas experts enter to check from one end to another end of the house, only at one of the toilets downstairs nearby to the kitchen they find a mixture of toilet bowl cleaner with liquid bath essence containing sulphur. 'This mixture causes the hydrogen sulphur gas- the most poisonous gas,' one of the gas experts says.

'Let us clear the gas from the house; meanwhile, please stay outside.'

Camelia is treated by an ambulance as she's given an oxygen mask to breathe the clean air to replace the poisonous gas entering her system.

Louise quickly helps the Professor up, pushes the hidden round button, and the floor underneath gives way. Automatically, the wooden staircase is visible, with Louise whispering and guiding him to climb down the stairs. Since he's invisible, no one will cure him except for Louise and Camelia. Once they reach the secret laboratory room, she places Professor Carlos on a dentist-like chair located in the inner part of the basement. Louise starts to search for items to remove the deadly gas.

On the notepad, it's written, Go to the cabinet at the edge of this room on the left to find stock of chlorination, water heater modification, activated carbon filtration, oxidizing filtration, or oxidizing chemical injection.

'Great!' Louise gets up and dashes to the designated spot for cabinets that keep all the tools and ingredients. Her eyes open widely with bewilderment that she can find most items in this basement.

Then she mixes them into a container, and once completed, she guides Professor Carlos to the mixture. 'Please put me in the small room located at the side; it is built with see-through glass, then release the ingredients for me to inhale. The only way to recover,' Professor Carlos writes.

Camelia calls out to Louise.

'Professor Carlos fainted by the gas smell; I'll be resuscitating him soon; you may join us at the basement,' Louise says.

'I will join you once I am settled with the police and gas experts,' Camelia replies.

After the ambulance is gone, the gas expert stays to ensure the house is completely clear from the poisonous gas, the police investigators come to find clues of the intruder's break-in, and evidence of fingerprints on the door, kitchen, and toilet are taken. The evidence of the bath soap and the toilet bowl cleaner that developed the gas is also being confiscated to find the culprits. It's about an hour or so until the investigators return.

Camelia appears at the basement laboratory while Louise is at the navigator button to revive Professor Carlos. Louise glares at Camelia.

Camelia notices Louise's upper eyelid, and both eyebrows are pulled together, and her mouth is stretched and drawn back. Her forehead is also creased into a frown, and at the same time, she bites her fingernails.

She faces the small glass cylinder room to find that the cylinder room is engulfed with a cloud of thick white smoke. In between it, she spots the glowing band Professor Carlos is wearing is flying up and down like he's struggling.

Then, there are suddenly a few flickers of lightning and thunder between the thick smoke. Then Professor Carlos's face and the whole body can be seen clearly. Initially, a full human face gradually became bigger before turning to its normal size.

Within a few seconds, his face turns puffy; then his skin grows bit by bit from his forehead, cheeks, chin, and then his hands. Finally, his mouth and eyes open wide for both Camelia and Louise.

Louise starts to panic. 'Should I reverse or stop the chemical neutralisation agents from flowing into there?' Louise asks herself.

Professor Carlos's hands are wailing high up, slapping the glass wall hard, his mouth is uttering ...he appears to be suffocating.

Suddenly, the basement laboratory electric supply is cut off.

'Oh no!' Louise and Camelia say at the same time. Camelia, who is holding her mobile, instantly grabs several icons and manages to click the torch one, and it shines directly on Louise, which makes her squint, then Camelia shifts the light to shine toward the glass room. They cannot see the Professor anywhere.

They're about to walk forward to peep the glass through the cylinder room when the laboratory lights are on by themselves. 'This is super weird,' Camelia says aloud.

'Let's look for him from outside first, to be safe. So let's start peeping from this point circle three hundred and sixty degrees around the cylinder.'

Louise nods.

They put their feet forward when the lights at the laboratory start flickering for a few minutes. 'This flickering is making me feel dizzy,' Camelia says. They head for the cylinder, and upon reaching it, the light resumes as usual. 'That is better,' Camelia says while looking at the lights on the ceiling.

Both stare out from their initial spot until three hundred and sixty degrees; both search for the Professor high and low but are unable to. 'Can you see his clothes anywhere or the glowing band?' Camelia asks Louise.

'Negative,' Louise replies.

'Wait!' Camelia shouts at Louise as she's about to open the handle of the cylinder. 'Please, let's wear this protective gas mask before opening the door; we just don't know what chemicals are lingering in the air.'

When Louise touches the handle, the Professor's face – half-human, half rubber – hits the glass wall, his eyes opening widely. Then, in the spur of the moment, a manhole via the ceiling of the cylinder is visible, and strong wind and smoke wafts through it, so strong that it causes the Professor's head and body to wobble.

Camelia and Louise's eyes are wide open upon witnessing this. 'This is bizarre; there should be a mad scientist doing since several changes to the Professor's features. We need to find them to stop this madness.'

Within seconds, the Professor is sucked into the manhole, and after then, it disappears into thin air.

They both blink and then stare at the gaping hole. Next, they approach the cylinder wall to take a closer look at the manhole, however, the ceiling looks clear.

Hurriedly, Louise opens the door concurrently, the lights of the room automatically on. She cautiously enters the glass room and sees the notepad on the floor, with a note scrawled there reading, 'Help!' She flips over the page, scientific chemical physics, digital technology combined and reads, 'Save me!'

Louise shouts at the edge of the door, 'Camelia, get me the latex gloves, tong, and Bunsen; it's at the longish table beside the big monitor.'

'Ok, sure,' Camelia replies.

She quickly collects all the items for Louise. Louise uses the gloves, takes the tong, and picks up some specimens.

There are pieces of green sticky rubber on the ground; she picks it up and places it into a transparent container. Next, she notices a small steel rod and a piece of fur beside a chair.

Once Louise is out from the cylinder, she says, 'This is weird; the fur looks similar to the creature's fur we caught that day,' Louise says to Camelia. 'Let me make a study on the molecules of both items. Very peculiar.'

Camelia looks bewildered by Louise's statement.

'Aha…as per my hunch…this fur is made from a few thousand molecules and electrons, then she pours investigation chemicals, the fur turns to…the same findings as to the creature. Never before seen in any animals,' Louise utters.

'Does this mean the creature came to visit the Professor? Or did the Professor momentarily change himself into the creature whilst he was in the midst of changing to a rubber face and disappear into thin air?' Camelia says.

'Or he's the monstrous creature eating people's hearts out,' both Camelia and Louise say simultaneously.

***

'How time flies, it's pitch black outside. Let me lock his house since there's no one home,' Camelia says.

A low growling sound appears from nearby.

'What is that?' Louise asks. They turn their heads left to the centre then to the right, searching for the sound. Then an enormous figure shadow is visible from afar, amongst the bushes and trees in front of them, causing the hair at the back of Camelia's neck to stand up.

They start walking, then continue to run even though their leg muscles to tighten. Camelia activates the nearest route to her house. 'Turn to the left to the shophouse's lot,' Camelia says after referring to waze application.

When they are walking, the air is being silent. There are dim lights coming from each of the shops in front of their porch. There are also neighbours jogging along this route, which makes Camelia feels safer.

A few minutes later, once they have passed the shop houses and require to walk into a quiet alley to go to Camelia's neighbourhood, a shadow that grows bigger can be seen lurking among the bushes and trees.

'Who is there?' Camelia asks while switching on her torch.

A high-pitched sound comes from above their heads.

'Run…Run..' Camelia pulls Louise's hand in order to run at the same speed.

'Ouch!' Camelia falls. Louise pulls her back to her feet.

After running a few blocks, sighing heavily with their hearts beating faster, they fall onto a dustbin. 'Ouch! Get up quick!' Louise says.

Within thirty minutes, they reach Camelia's neighbourhood, and it's brightly lit with streetlights. Two or three couples are jogging, who smile at them as they pass. The shadow and sound die down temporarily.

'I recognise this corner and trees; my house should be just a few feet away.' Camelia says.

They're both appalled and blink in disbelief.' Where is my

house?' Camelia's hands start to tremble.

'Maybe it's on the wrong lane? I'm not sure this house is your neighbour,' Louise says.

They're standing at the side of the pavement and turn their faces in the opposite direction, passing the small field in the centre to find Camelia's house.

'Look,' Camelia says, pointing. 'Three blocks away from here is Mr Bucket's house. Therefore, my house must be behind his.'

'Let's go!' Louise says.

Suddenly, a screeching noise appears above their heads.

Louise looks upward while Camelia pulls her by the wrist, urging her to move.

'Looks like it has tail…a monkey?' Louise says.

It jumps, scampers, and makes a lot of noises, moving from one roof to another.

It starts scraping the neighbour's roof. It's noisy, which causes them to go and check it out.

'Keep quiet, you little beast! Get out! Get out!' Mrs. Daisy shouts.

She takes out her long gun and shoots in the direction the sound is coming from. Suddenly, the neighbourhood is silent. Nothing happens.

Within seconds, a huge creature jumps onto Mrs. Daisy, topples her with its heavyweight, and Mrs. Daisy is unable to break free.

Camelia and Louise's mouths open widely. Camelia notices the gun is placed on the ground, and runs as fast as she can toward it, picks it up, checks the bullets before storming toward the creature. Before she manages to shoot it, the creature runs away.

While Camelia storms toward it, the creature who overpowered Mrs. Daisy manages to bite her chest, and his sharp claws and heavy paw tear out her heart in the nick of time. He's holding her heart with blood dripping here and there at the neighbourhood route when he speeds off.

They approach Mrs. Daisy's lifeless body, wishing they could have saved her.

There's a large hole in the centre of her chest, which looks like a butcher has dug an electric knife cutter into her chest.

Firstly, a drill has removed her chest bones, then scraps veins at all sides of the heart, which is missing. Her eyes stare up in anguish. She didn't die peacefully.

They don't watch the scene for long as a new attacker has crept up behind them and smacks them over their heads, plunging them into darkness.

CHAPTER 13

'**I** won't be able to sleep over tonight since I have my mother's surprise birthday party. My sister is organising it at her house. You'll be OK by yourself, won't you?' Louise asks Camelia.

'Oh yes, I have to submit my Information Systems project by Thursday morning, so I'll be a little tied up in finalising my research, typing, and re-editing,' Camelia replies.

They head for a T junction where they have to part with each other since Louise is going to her home at Rose Road, which is on the left side of the T junction, whereas Camelia's house is located on Burns Road.

'Please give your mum my happy birthday greetings,' says Camelia before they separate.

Clouds begin to dance away from the sky. Daylight starts to drain away as they split off into different directions.

A gust of icy wind passes and makes her shudder when she steps onto her neighbourhood.

A few minutes from her walk, she passes Mrs. Daisy's house, where flowers and a note of condolence are placed on her veranda. Suddenly, Camelia recalls the unfortunate incident, and her heart is filled with sadness. 'When can this be over?' she says to herself.

She reaches her house a few steps from Mrs. Daisy's house and twists the doorknob. 'Is that you, Gummy?' Camelia shouts.

Then the surroundings become silent.

'Well, it must be the neighbour's cat wandering around the neighbourhood,' Camelia says to herself whilst pushing the door open. She steps into her house, switches on the hallway lights, closes, locks the door behind her, and then presses her password to activate the security alarm on the alarm keypad.

After dinner, she starts to concentrate on doing her research via the internet in her room. Four books she borrowed on her Information Systems syllabus from her neighbourhood library are removed from her backpack. She flips the books open, scanning one page to another to find details for her to include in her project paper.

An antique clock in her living room has been chiming four times since dinner, indicating it as midnight...

Whilst she is typing the last chapter, the drumming sound she heard before returns from the direction of her mother's room. The sound grows louder in Camelia's ear. She pushes aside her chair, walks toward her vanity table, and pulls the middle drawer to take out a huge earphone. She puts it over her head and blasts music in her ear. Ignoring the noise, she continues typing her project paper for an hour. Then, when she begins to feel tired, she leaves her study table and falls flat on her tummy on the edge of her bed, with her arms over her head. She doesn't even manage to change to her pyjamas or brush her teeth.

When the antique clock chimes at three in the morning, Camelia cries out,' Ouch!' Her eyes jolt open as she falls on the floor. 'What time is it?' The drumming sounds resonate as she's about to get up from the floor.

This time the drum sound is as loud as a microphone in her ear. 'Ouch! This is too loud.' She got up from the floor, grabs her pillow and covers both ears while rocking her body to and fro on the bed, trying to withhold the annoyance of the sound. 'Argh!' Her cheek turns red as rage grips her. She feels her anger overpowering her emotions, gets up from the bed, crosses the room to her vanity table on the middle drawer, and plans to take out the chef's knife she was hiding there before. As she pulls the drawer, she cannot find the knife.

This time the drumming sound repeats itself every few seconds.

Her heart beats so fast it nearly leaps out of her chest.

Then she opens the top drawer, and to her relief, the chef knife is kept there in a small container. She takes off its cover, then removes it, feeling more confident with the knife in her hand. She starts walking to her door. While she's about to turn her knob, a gust of strong wind blows past her face, which leads her room door to open wide.

She turns to look back at her room; all the windows are tightly closed.

She breathes in deeply and suddenly feels cold, pulls her light jacket to close her chest then continues walking. Once she steps outside her room, the drumming sound dies. She strains her eyes to look at her mother's room for any lights or shudders, but there's none. Then, as she's about to re-enter her bedroom, the sound begins again. It repeats every few seconds. Finally, she determines to investigate it, confident it's coming from her mother's room.

She twists the doorknob, listens for the noise; however, it's silent. So she opens the door widely, switches on the room's lights, and the room is neat and untouchable. Everything is quiet…

She walks further in to check the windows at the opposite of the spot she's standing; the windows appear locked at her spot.

'I'm often suspicious of this window and the table underneath it. If I don't check it thoroughly with my own eyes, I'll regret and unable to find the truth.' Due to that she takes one step a time, and reaches the window about a hundred meters away from the table. As she stands beside the table, she notices it looks neat but is filled with piles of paperwork. The windows remain still. Camelia looks through the window, only seeing the night sky aglow with bright street lights. Nothing mystifying.

The drumming sound comes again, but this time it's not within her mother's room. She momentarily stops walking further and tries to locate the direction of the sound. Subsequently, she turns to face the door that remains ajar, and walks across the room toward the door as her right foot steps out.

The sound has now increased, filling Camelia with fear.

Confidently this time, she raises the chef's knife, preparing to defend herself from any foresee attacks. *You can do it, Cam; you are Tae Kwando certified; you can easily overturn your opponent.*' She inhales deeply to release her fear.

Rapidly she stomps out of her mum's room.

This time the sound is coming from…her room? She runs at top speed while holding the chef knife, and once she reaches her room, she places her ear to her door, but she is unable to hear anything.

Suddenly, the noise appears again. Then the house is in silent for a while. 'This is ridiculous. I'm going back to sleep!'

As she twists her room's doorknob, the noise continuously resounds, making Camelia decide to walk down the staircase. She switches on her mobile torch, since the downstairs floor is in darkness.

When her last feet steps onto the ground floor, the drum sounds become louder and she steps further, passing the living room. The sound is dimmer here, so she proceeds further, passing by the kitchen. She stops momentarily in the kitchen area as the sound stops where she's standing. Sigh. She switches on the dim dining lights located just beside the kitchen. She opens the fridge door when suddenly she sees a man's silhouette passing in front of her.

Quickly she closes the fridge door and follows the direction of the silhouette. She lingers, wondering what to do next.

This time, it comes from the study room.

'Code Red,' she texts Louise via WhatsApp.

'Her heart beats faster as she reaches the door, and she breathes in deeply, feeling confident. She twists the doorknob and opens the door initially just an inch, then another, and then her head goes in. She sees nothing and feels braver; her left-hand grapples the wall beside the door panel to press the switch, which causes the room to become brighter. She's about to touch the mousepad when suddenly the screen blacks out.

She turns her head to face a book rack the size of a door.

One particular glowing book catches her attention with blueish light. Her eyes widen with interest. She quickly wakes from the chair at the computer table and approaches the book rack.

A thudding solid sound resonates. The drum sounds seem to follow the glowing light.

The sound stops. The glowing light disappears into thin air.

Her mouth opens widely. Just as I'm about to reach out and touch it, it's gone. Unbelievable!

The lights in the room turn back to normal. Camelia blinks, staring at a blank white wall.

She blinks again. Her right-hand moves to the left. 'Ouch!' Her fingers pinch her left hand hard. 'OK, I'm not sleepwalking, right?' Then she touches the blank wall, starting from the furthest left side of the imaginary book rack she envisions, the centre, and then to the right.

'Cam, where are you?' Louise shouts.

Camelia smiles to herself, turns, and walks away quickly to greet her friend.

She twists the doorknob, pushes the door forward, however it feels heavy, as though there's a strong wind trying to pull from within the room. It's too heavy, but there's a small opening in the door.

'Help! I'm here!' Camelia shouts at Louise.

The door slams shut in her face. The thudding starts to re-echo through the room.

The book rack re-appears, a heavy oldish leather book appears in the centre of all other books. It opens a few pages quickly then flips by itself, pages by pages until it reaches the centre of the book. Then the glowing blueish light shines brightly, and its source is from the book, which blinds Camelia.

Then the strong gust of wind pulls Camelia toward the book's direction. Camelia grabs the tip of the table; with her strength, she pulls herself inwards toward the computer table; however, the wind current is powerful and causes her hands to let go. Finally, she's blown away, absorbs and disappears into the book.

After a few minutes, Camelia tumbles.

Camelia opens her eyes… she's covered in sand…

'Where am I?' she says once but her voice echoes.

She closes her eyes.' I must be dreaming…please let it be a dream.'

Then she opens them. 'Ooh…Ooh!' I feels fear, worried I'm alone in this new place.

The ceiling appears as though it's made of stones mixed with sand, not her bedroom's ceiling. She gets up from where she is lying, skimming the space to identify her whereabouts.

She seems to be in a cave.

'You fools, walk faster,' a harsh, husky voice shouts.

Camelia quickly finds shelter, and fortunately for her, there's a huge rock located a hundred metres away from her, so she tiptoes there. She's afraid to make any noise, unsure where she is and who they are.

'We are to find a lady with a diamond shape digital chip,' someone says nervously from nearby.

Gulp...the diamond shape is a chip...I wonder why it's planted onto certain people, like Lucas and myself. Suddenly goosebumps on her skin are visible as she starts to feel fear like her life is in perilous danger.

'Yes.' Camelia hears a smacking noise, the sound of one of them hitting the other? 'This is for failing to get the lady.' Sweat starts trickling from her forehead, and her hands start trembling. They seem to be quite fierce; how can I escape? Camelia thinks.

'But...but...Ms. Pediburp, we're positive it's the correct lady, RFID chip detector will ever never go wrong.'

They pass the rock without noticing Camelia's footprints on the sand. Camelia holds her breath as she notices her footprints just a few metres away from the path the three people are walking along. She manages to peep and sees two dwarf-like men with moustaches and a skinny old figure, but she can't determine whether they are male or female.

After ten minutes or so, Camelia returns to the spot where she landed and starts shovelling the sand to find the chef knife she was holding while being swallowed by the wind and the book. When she uncovers it, she hides it in her jacket pocket. She sees some pebbles beside it and takes some in her hands if she requires them for her escape.

'Now I need to know where I am, how I get here, and how I return home?' Camelia says to herself. As she's thinking, she sees the footprints made by the three people. Maybe I can find something by following this trail. But, before starting, let me check out my mobile to see if there is any network.

Camelia isn't far from the location of the three people, and she's able to see their route. They're heading east toward a blank stone wall.

One of the dwarf-sized men takes out something that looks like a remote control. Then an opening from the walls of the caves starts to shake and gradually opens upward.

Seeing this, her eyes open widely, then she rubs them. I think I'm dreaming.

Once it opens, Camelia squints her eyes. The place on the other side appears like water. 'Why are they entering a place surrounded with water....sea. Are they mermaids?'

'Wait a minute,' she says to herself.

Within a split second, Camelia rushes to pass the invisible door and ensures the three people don't notice her, walk closely behind them between the rocks. As she tries to step over the door, she feels water splashes over her face and is unable to breathe. She quickly retracts her steps in the nick of time, before the cave's wall closes.

Her face is drenched with water. Her bangs are wet.

Bang...bang...

***

The alarm clock screeches, and she wakes with a start.

'Where am I?' Camelia opens her eyes, sees her room ceiling, blinks …turns her head to face the alarm clock placed on the side table. 'Don't tell me it's just a dream again!'

She doesn't know what to think. It all feels real – the water, the sand, and the three creepy-looking people. Was it real, or was it all a strange dream?

CHAPTER 14

'Cam, I'll be away for two weeks for work at my client's office; therefore, I won't be coming down for two weekends,' Camelia's mother says over the phone.

'Mum, is it near the Head Quarters that you're working?'

'I'll let you know once I have the details,' her mother says before abruptly hanging up.

She starts dialing Louise mobile number. 'Hello, Louise. I feel something strange is happening to Mum. I received a call which indicates her name on my phone but the lady's voice at the end didn't sound like her at all. It sounded raucous and toneless. Totally different from my mother's, with her sweet voice. I'm worried.'

'Hmm, let's make a surprise visit,' Louise suggests.

Camelia is pleased with this idea. 'Let's plan it soon.' Camelia replies while sounding cheerful.

***

'This is our checklist for the visit:

- Honda Civic bluish car
- Backpack – light clothes/ bubble-gum
- Electric knife cutter
- Flip baton

'Hooray! We're ready for an adventure!' Louise shouts.

After four hours of driving in the car, they stop at a motel for the night.

'A room for two, please,' Camelia says to the receptionist. 'Is it this quiet on the highway and town toward the Davensworkpicks?'

The receptionist shudders, and her face turns ashen. Her finger points at Camelia to come closer. 'Heard that whoever enters will never return, a secret, please.' Camelia's eyes open widely, and she hugs herself tightly for protection. She whispers, chuckles, and cracks up laughing. 'Just kidding, enjoy your stay, ladies,' she continues. Camelia and Louise smile nervously.

I wonder if the city that Mum is working is safe and people are friendly. Will it be easy to meet her, or will she ignore us? I suppose once we reach her office, I will make a call and say to Mum that we are here to complete our project and we require a change of environment, so visiting her for a short while wouldn't cause too much trouble.

The next day, on the road, Camelia says,' Hmm this is

interesting, according to Waze, we have to drive through a forest to get there since the highway is blocked by fallen trees which have caused a truck to overturn.' Camelia sighs. 'OK, we turn around toward the forest lane then, and we follow the Ford car in front; I think he's going in the same direction as us.'

There is a tapping sound on the window. 'Let me check your driver's license please, ladies,' a police officer with a toothpick sticking out of his mouth says. 'So what are your plans, and how long are you staying here, young ladies?' he says after they show him the papers.

Camelia and Louise glance at each other with wide eyes. What a weird question to ask from an officer? Is this town restricted for certain visitors?

'We are here for a change of environment because we have to write our project papers for the weekend,' Louise lies.

'Alright. You may enter the town.' He presses the button on the device in his hands, and the barrier next to the security post rises.

After passing the security, their car enters the town. 'Wow, it looks super clean, and there are many skyscrapers,' says Louise. 'So where is your Mum's office?'

'Let's make a surprise visit,' says Camelia.

'Is she having a romance with her boss, and that's why she can't visit you at home?' says Louise with a chuckle.

'Let me check out the Waze application for any design company nearby.' says Louise while her fingers start to fumble the application. 'Ehmm, there is none.'

'Why not we stop here at this Café Ben, people who work

in it will be able to tell us something; what do you think?' Camelia suggests. 'No harm in trying. Let me park the car at the designated parking space opposite the café.'

'Hi there, two English tea, please. By the way, we are searching for a Design Company or advertising Company in this town, can you guide us?' Camelia asks the person at the counter.

'I am sorry I am a student here just shifted a few weeks back, and I am yet to know my surroundings.' She replies.

Sigh.

Once done with their drinking, they got into the car and drive towards a motel. While they stop at the traffic light junction...

'Eh! Stop the car quick! Did you see Ben, Mum's co-worker? He must be assisting her at her new office,' Camelia says excitedly.

'No, why don't we follow him, he may lead us to Casendra faster,' Louise says as she turns the wheel to the right to follow him. He's walking fast with three cups of coffee in his right arm and an iPad on another, earphones in his ears.

They honk the horn. Ben turns his head toward the sound of the car honking.

'Hi Ben, remember us?' Louise pulls down the car window.

Ben smiles nervously, 'Hi, what are you both doing here?' His lips tighten.. 'We are busy around the clock; the richest client is making us work twenty-four hours a day; he's insane! I don't think it's wise that you visit your mother right now; it will only make her more stressed. She has been throwing tantrums by shouting at us and throwing books and papers on us if we don't find the solutions timely enough.'

'Oh, alright, we'll be on our way; please promise not to mention us at all to my mother. Otherwise, she will be angry at me.' Camelia says in her sweetest voice.

'Yes, sure.' Ben replies.

Louise hears this and blinks. She closes her window then and snaps, 'Are you nuts! We are already here, so close to seeing Casendra, and we drove for hours to get here!' Louise pounds her fist on the steering wheel.

'I have a plan; we will sneak out tonight, we will be the 'spy',' Camelia says.

'No way, they have to work around the clock as graphic designers; they aren't researchers right?' Louise says with a smile.

***

The clock chimes to ten at night, and both Camelia and Louise are ready to investigate while wearing their black slacks and light-dark blue jackets, with matching black masks over their noses so they will be harder to identify if they're caught.

They park their car a few metres away from the twenty-five storey office buildings with tinted glass. 'According to the directory, Mum's office should be on the eighth floor.' Camelia shows Louise. They leave the car, and are about to approach the building when a huge explosion shakes it, and they are forced to balance themselves to stop falling. Please …

please… The explosion shouldn't be at Mum's office…. I hope it isn't hers. Will she be alright?

Suddenly, the building is shaken by the explosion's impact, causing glass to be thrown out and shattered in the air. Within a few minutes, the building falls flat like a pancake. Its foundation, floors, roofs, ceilings, and the top floor cave in and crumble to the ground. There is debris flying everywhere, and smoke grows thicker around them. People in the buildings are frantic, running here and there to save their lives.

'911, we have an emergency- a building has collapsed -please send an ambulance and fire brigade,' Louise says into her phone.

Camelia's mouth drops open, and her hands are on her forehead as she stumbles down on the roadside. "Mama! Mama! Please don't leave me alone!' Tears roll down her face as she screams, fear tightening her chest and making it difficult to breathe. Thinking of her mother crushed and trapped in the building, I cannot live without Mum. She's the only family I have left.

Louise pulls Camelia away from the roadside and wraps her arms around Camelia's shoulders for added comfort.

Suddenly, Louise notices a white van park a hundred metres from the collapsed building with two dwarf-sized men are pushing and carrying a stretcher with a lifeless woman lying on it. Camelia can only see her mother's auburn shoulder-length hair from where they're standing, but the sight makes her want to scream.

'Wait!' Louise points at the white van. 'The van doesn't

look like a typical ambulance,' she says.

Quickly turning her head to look, surprised by her friend's statement, Camelia runs as fast as she can toward the van without thinking or looking, with Louise following behind her. From this distance, she can just make out a hand with mole on it on the limp woman's form. Once they reach the spot where the van was temporarily parked, it speeds off before they can chase it. 'I can't keep up; the van is too fast,' Camelia says. She sees something broken left on the road; she picks it up. It's a pair of blue framed spectacles, similar to her mother's, but they are broken in half. 'She cannot see without her glasses; her vision power is quite high,' Camelia says, with her forehead creased into a frown. 'What do they want with my mother?' As she clenches her fists as anger starts to develop within her.

'Cam, please calm down. Let's ask the authority of the building. Maybe they have updates on the whereabouts of those people. I hope your mother is on her way to her hotel - call it a day, and she misses the building collapse tragedy. I don't think anyone wants to harm your sweet mother.' Louise tries to comfort Camelia.

'Hello Ben, are you OK?' Louise says into her phone, taking Camelia by surprise. She listens closely, trying to hear the man's words before Louise can repeat them for her.

'I... I'm OK; I'm just lucky I went back before the building collapsed. Camelia, I'm so sorry, but the authorities haven't been able to locate your mother anywhere in the debris,' Ben says via the phone. 'Please let me know if I can help any further.'

'Listen, Ben, we saw two very short men place my mother onto a stretcher and place her into a white van and drive off,' Camelia says nervously.

'Are you sure it wasn't an ambulance, you know your great grandmother is the famous millionaire's Professor Ezra Daclan, and the company might have given her the special treatment for being her daughter,' Ben adds.

My great grandmother is long gone and forgotten; will anyone still remember her to give VIP treatment to Mum? I doubt it, Camelia thinks to herself.

'I feel deep inside that there's something fishy going on, and I'd like us to investigate it ourselves. Ben, please, I need your help to find the records of the street video surveillance around the building, especially a hundred metres away at the back. Let me activate FaceTime so you can see the location where my mother was last seen. Also, please check all the hospitals. I want to know if there's a possibility that Mum was checked in, if they are the good guys,' Camelia adds.

'OK Camelia, I will WhatsApp you the updates; if there is anything else you need me to do, please call me and stay away from danger.'

They enter their car, and Louise starts to twist the car key in the ignition. 'Why are the exhaust and car engine sounds whirring so loudly? Is the sound coming from our car?' Camelia asks.

Louise reverses the car onto a lane.

'Did you hear that?' There is a crash nearby, and broken glass can be heard near the corner, accompanying with a loud smash. Camelia opens the car door and runs in the direction of the noise. 'It sounded as though the van is overturned; if it's the van my mother is in, hopefully, she isn't injured; I need to save her badly,' Camelia says with fear pounding in her heart.

Louise manages to catch up with her around twenty-five metres away from Camelia. Once they reach the scene, Louise snatches Camelia aside to hide behind a large oak tree. Camelia struggles to break free. Louise whispers, 'We don't know if the guys are good people; we are here to save your mother Casendra and not be captured ourselves.'

Camelia nods.

Louise takes out her mobile and starts recording the scene. They're watching the two dwarf-sized men carrying a lifeless lady in an oxygen mask covered with a blanket. Then a green metallic Volvo car brakes beside them and opens the door.

'Come in quickly!' a woman's husky voice can be heard. Instantly, two men and the unconscious woman are pushed into the car, the door yet to be closed, and the car is driving at top speed.

From her spot, Camelia notices the lady's wrist contains the butterfly bracelet she gave her mother last year for good luck. It is confirmed, they are kidnapping her mother, and Camelia is both terrified and heartbroken. I must save her.

'I got it, the video footage of the culprit. We're able to nail them down in no time,' Louise says.

'I managed to take a photo of the car plate,' Camelia adds.

'Oh my god, the dwarf sized men! They're so familiar.'

'What a freak! They are the men I saw at the sandy caves; the wall absorbed me at the study room in my house;

their height and features are exactly the same, don't tell me there is someone behind this kidnapping? Both my great grandmother and my mother!' Camelia's voice sounds stern while she punches her other hand.

Camelia thinks, *I guess my mother and great grandmother have a secret that the kidnappers require. What shall we do to save them?* We need to hurry. Camelia's right-hand touches her forehead, and she shakes her head whilst her left-hand grasps the tip of her blouse and crumples it.

CHAPTER 15

H ello Camelia, it's me, Bob from the FBI speaking. I would like to share the video footage of someone kidnapping Lucas's corpse and the fate of Dr. David Tzo with Dr Alicia Scwerzerzof. Let me know if you recognise the kidnapper.'

'Who would want to steal a dead body? Especially he is just an ordinary student,' says Camelia.

It's worthless,' Bob says.

'Unless there is something valuable being kept in the body, and now the culprit requires it,' Camelia says.

Then Camelia and Louise watch the video that Bob sent over.

A man dresses as the courier serviceman with a cap covering parts of his eyes and covers his mouth with a greyish cotton surgical mask. He pushes a heavy-duty hand trolley cart with his hand gripping the integral carry handle and places down some stacks of envelopes to camouflage his real identity. From the video, there is audio that Camelia and Louise can hear,' Hey mate, dropping off some envelopes here.'

'Sure …sign here ..where is Mike today?' Officer Daniel asks.

'I'm using the gents, yeah, mate.' He walks to the gents to hide.

As indicated on his badge, the man whose name is Rock walks out from the gents and changes his courier service uniform to an officer uniform.

Then, he turns to the left, walks further inward, and takes out a box size of a matchbox, a one hundred metre from the CCTV, pointing in its direction to change the view as serene and non-habitant. Once it changes, he confidently walks past the CCTV and pushes the emergency door to reveal the laboratory area.

When he enters, he sees two doctors. There is a hidden CCTV that managed to capture this footage.

'I got an instruction that you both require my assistance to move a valuable item. We didn't call for help. Maybe there is a mistake. By the way, this is a restricted area officer. What can we do for you?' says Dr. David Tzo, with Dr. Alicia Scwerzerzof beside him. Both doctors appear suspicious since no officers are allowed in the research area except for the FBI.

'Not going out for lunch, doctors?' Rocks says to distract them while heading in their direction with a thick wooden baton in his right hand. He stops fifty metres from their spot, then continues talking, 'The FBI will be coming shortly for any latest findings to be shared.' Then he presses a small orange button on the baton, a black arrow dart with tranquilliser in it is released in Dr David Tzo's direction which hits him on his neck and he immediately falls down and smacks his head against the steel research table.

Dr. Alicia gasps with horror quickly inserts chemicals into an empty syringe before throwing it in Rocks' direction.

It falls just a few steps away from Rocks, and his eyes widen, but his ears grow red with anger. With his muscular body and firm fist, he grabs hold of Dr. Alicia, puts his shoulder and arms around her neck, and pulls and chokes her. Rocks whispers in her ear, 'I'll spare your life if you give me Lucas's corpse.'

With that, Rocks releases his firm grip slightly on Dr. Alicia's neck to allow her to breathe.

'Lucas? He's in the steel cabinet beside our research table,' she stammers.

'Where are the keys?' Rocks says sternly.

'In my research jacket hanging over there.' She tries to wriggle free from Rocks' grip to show the direction. Rocks understands and releases his grip slightly, giving Dr. Alicia the chance to kick his groin with her blue heels.

'Ouch!' he shouts.

As Dr. Alicia is about to walk to the side to press for emergency help, Rocks is fast in his action, shoots Dr. Alicia in the back of her head, and falls to the floor. Rocks quickly puts his hand into her pocket to retrieve the keys and uses them to open the steel cabinet. He pulls the trolley tray from the cabinet, unzips the corpse to check his face. Then, he starts to carry the corpse. It's heavy since Lucas is -built muscularly, and the doctors embalmed his body to preserve it for the investigation. Rocks' face grows redder, and sweat trickles down his forehead as he tries to withhold the heavyweight of the corpse. Thereafter, he places Lucas onto a black nylon bag on top of the trolley, then places Dr. Alicia's body into the steel cabinet and locks it. He throws the bunch of keys into the dustbin nearby, muttering, 'Good riddance.'

He pushes the trolley as fast as he can through the exit door. Someone must be assisting him since the door latch is unleashed automatically. The van driver drives as fast as a Formula 1 driver, just in time for Rocks to push and pull the corpse into the back of the van. He jumps onto the back, closes the door behind him as there are a couple of officers shooting in the direction of their van. One bullet manages to go into the left front tyres, which causes the van to screech to a halt, nearly skidding in the process. With his skilful gadget operator, the driver releases a spare glide tyre to replace the punctured tyre so their transportation can proceed to safety.

'The guy's features are similar to the person's I saw in the cave and who kidnapped Mum, but I cannot share this information with Bob yet since I have no concrete evidence,' Camelia says to Louise. 'Oh my, if he is the one, we can put him in behind bars.' Louise replies.

***

'How to rescue my mother?' Camelia shouts while walking to and fro in the motel.

Her phone rings, and she places it to her ear. 'Cam, it's

Ben here; none of the hospitals nearby have any patients named Casendra.'

'I knew all this while this is foul play,' Camelia says.

On their way back to their hometown, Camelia says, 'Who wants Mum so badly? 'Let's make a list.'

A) Someone whose great grandmother may have an argument / enemy

(she seems fierce and stern from the family photos)

B) Mum's previous boss- maybe he has an answer on clients etc

C) Mum's romance? Not even once has she ever mentioned my father or anyone else. She often brushes the subject aside when I ask her about it.

Solutions to gather the information:

A) To interview Ms. Reeta, great grandmother's previous secretary

B) To interview Gary, great grandmother's private driver

C) To interview and investigate Casendra previous and current bosses / clients

D) To search great grandmother's house to ransack Casendra's room to find further information about her lover.

'We go the top of the list first', to the International Research Foundation Department. '

'Hi, Ms. Reeta, I'm Camelia, the granddaughter of

Professor Ezra Daclan.'

'Oh my, you are real? I have been waiting for this moment to see you in person; you know how the Professor is secretive about her personal life.' She is on speakerphone, so Louise also hears it.

'Are you available for us to meet up today?' Camelia asks.

'Yes, after office hours at the Huckleberry Café near the corner next to Booknext stores at 5 PM?'

'See you there,' Camelia replies.

***

Camelia and Louise are drinking tea at Huckleberry's when Ms. Reeta wears a greenish-brown blazer. She's tanned with a long ponytail, and appears in her forties. 'Hi!' They all shake hands.

'How beautiful you have grown up to be; you resemble your mother,' she says.

'Thanks,' Camelia replies.

'Professor Ezra Daclan has become a control freak over your mother due to her daughter's death, Celia (it is Casendra's mother). Celia died when some research went wrong; Professor Ezra's right-hand assistant, another Professor from the Netherlands, carelessness, which caused the laboratory to burn down in a gulf of smoke with Celia in it. Your mother wasn't allowed to go near any science and research centers or projects due to fear of repeating history. She was supposed to tie the knot...,' her voice trails off suddenly as her face hits the table with blood flowing around her like syrup.

'Reeta…Reeta, are you OK?' Camelia asks while tilting Reeta's head to one side.

Then there is a crash, and the window they're seated beside breaks into a million pieces as the bullet hits the window and fires straight into Ms. Reeta's neck.

'Duck down quickly!' Louise shouts at Camelia. They bend down and crawl underneath the table, and another bullet flies above their heads and hits a waitress who drops dead on the floor. Their heartbeats start to pound faster, and Camelia feels uneasy as she's unable to breathe. They crawl in high-speed to the back of the café to escape.

Camelia and Louise scamper and fling the back kitchen door wide open, get up and smoothen out their attire. 'We're so close to dying,' Louise says nervously. Camelia nods. Her face is as pale as the wall paint.

'Next, we must meet Gary, Ezra's driver, for further information. Someone must have known we are investigating and tries to put an end in us finding out what they're trying to hide.'

They reach the park, where the car's brake stops. 'How do you suppose we find this Gary guy without any clues or landmarks?' Louise adds.

A message comes in, and it reads, 'Meet me at the bench next to a yellow ice cream stall. I'm the man with a white beard and white curly hair wearing a checked shirt in red and black stripes.'

'OK, see you soon,' Camelia replies.

'I have something to pass to you,' Gary adds.

'I am just wondering if there is someone who doesn't want

me to know the real findings, and that is why Ms. Reeta was shot dead? I wonder if Gary will be the next meal in their menu,' Camelia says loudly.

'I have the deepest feeling we are close to solving this mystery,' Louise adds with a smile.

As described, they sit down on the bench, intrigued with the ice cream seller as he's singing aloud to attract customers. They turn their heads to look at the time and notice Gary is late by ten minutes. 'Is he coming or chickening out at the last minute?' Louise says sarcastically.

'Look at the twelve o clock direction, there's an old man fit with the description walking toward us, and he's smiling and nodding at us.'

'What's that envelope in his hands?' Louise says to Camelia.

'How are you doing, young ladies?' He nods and tilts his head in a clear sign of respect.

Camelia gets up to give him space to sit between them. Then Gary turns to look at Camelia and says, 'Excuse me for staring at you, you sure look like your mother. I remember driving her around to school, then to university. She has lots of admirers, especially the famous bright guy...what was his name? Chan.. Chang ...or was it, Lee? I can't recall his name that well, but he is good; in my opinion, he's the greatest competitor to your great grandmother Ezra. The Professor is getting older with a lack of new inventions in her initiatives; the guy posed a threat to the Professor to maintain her credentials and awards. So we must put a stop to...Chang... yes that is his surname. Now I remember she mentioned his name and her plans.'

'So what is the link between Chang and my great grandmother, with my mother kidnapped?' Camelia asks.

A silent rifle bullet suddenly fires straight into Gary's forehead, and Camelia and Louise scream, their shock never-ending. Streaming of blood flowing through the centre of his forehead, a small hole is visible in his forehead then his body falls to the ground. Passers-by see the blood and hear the gunshots start screaming their head off.

Camelia and Louise jolt and jump out from the bench, and hide behind the ice cream parlour mobile stall. Their hands are trembling, and Louise starts to cry. 'We are next; I don't want to die,' Camelia says while sneaking off to see if there are any suspicious people around.

Then she pushes Louise to the nearby bushes to hide. 'Oh! The envelope…Gary says he needs to give us something.' Camelia crawls to the bench, pushes Gary's hand aside since the envelope is under his armpit, grabs it quickly then crawls back into her hiding spot near the bushes.

They run away as police sirens come to a halt.

***

They're having lunch, eating, and talking. Camelia is observant, seeing Rocks, whom she recognizes from the video footage that the FBI Bob showed to them, is watching them for around twenty minutes while eating their chicken sandwiches at the side table beside a dustbin at Subway café for dinner. Feeling a bit nervous, however, continue to stay calm and look normal.

She bites her food a little, then gets up, takes her tray, and sits next to Rocks at an empty table. She tilts her head and says,' So when are you taking me to see my mother?

Rocks looks surprised and asks, 'What are you talking about? Mind your own business girl.'

A few minutes after Rocks leaves, Camelia and Louise finish their dinners, and as they're about to enter the car, Rocks grabs hold of Camelia and Louise, both of their legs were kicking Rocks' tummy and any other part of his body; however, he is strong, their kick undeterred him. He immediately ties their hands and places duct tape over their mouths roughly. Both girls were kicking to free themselves; however, Rocks is strong. He places them in his van. As Rocks is about to close the van door, Louise kicks Rocks on his nose, which causes him to bleed, and momentarily halts from closing the door when Louise rolls over and falls onto the parking cement. Louise moves inch by inch quickly to hide in the nearby bushes. 'That brat!' Instantly, he closes the van door and speeds away quickly.

'Hey, girl.' He places chloroform on Camelia's nose, and immediately she falls into a deep sleep. Upon reaching their destination, Camelia is placed in a sick bay. A few minutes pass, and being a strong-willed girl, she wakes on the steel hospital bed and starts walking around, bit by bit. However, since the chloroform is still lingering in her body and bloodstream, she cannot walk straight; she keeps falling but crawls nearer to the noises, determined.

She hears a man's voice saying, 'She is so beautiful after

all these years, my goddess, finally you two have done a good job.' He claps his hand several times, smiling from ear to ear. 'She is unconscious, right? Place her in my surgery room instantly; I need to do minor surgery in her armpit to take out the chip before she wakes. I wouldn't want her to feel any pain...my queen, my lover.'

Camelia hears the last word.. "queen,' which jolts her momentarily, thinking in her subconscious mind, Can it be Mum? She crouches and peeps. Her hands cover her mouth to prevent her from shouting at the sight she is seeing.

Casendra lifeless body is placed onto the surgery bed, and Dr Mark touches her lovely auburn locks, buttoning down his shirt until his navel, kissing her hands from the tip of her hands, licking little by little with his tongue, then repeatedly kissing her hands upper and upper toward her arms. A tall skinny lady (Mrs. Pediburp) accidentally drops a pen on the floor. Hearing the sound, suddenly his face turns red, and his jaw tightens, then he puts out his electronic detector to find the diamond shape chip he inserted the night before the fire brutally scarred his face.

'Marvellous… the chip is intact. Let's take it out.' Then, with his eyes full of rage, he's about to put surgical scissors into Camelia's mother's armpit when suddenly she turns her head, although her eyes remain closed and she groans, 'Ouch, my head is spinning.' Dr. Mark's eyes widen, realising Camelia's mother has beaten the tranquilliser fast.

'That is Mum's voice. I hope she is fine. What are they planning to do to her next?' Camelia thoughts.

Ms. Pediburp is fast to realise, and instantly refills the

tranquilliser syringe and injects it into Camelia's mother's neck. She looks lifeless again, her hand falling away from her forehead. Dr. Mark's shirt is wet with his sweat as he isn't expecting his love to look so stunning when he's about to do surgery on her.

This time Camelia's eyes widen when she hears the word chips. She quickly realises she's about to expose herself by squatting in front of the transparent door and instantly moves aside to hide. She peers through into the room and can hear a man and another hoarse voice talking.

'I can't do it, Mrs. Pediburp, I'll hand over to you, get the chip out from her armpit. Please be gentle when removing the chip, and make sure she's under anaesthesia. Then place her into the crystal room, and please remember to treat her as my queen.' Dr. Mark walks away, stealing a final look at her mother before he goes. He shouts, 'I need the chip fast!'

Ms Pediburp gasps. 'Right on, boss!

Instantly a man in a doctor's white uniform named Dr. Mark with his half face covered with a steel mask, storm out from the door. Camelia holds her breath to ensure she isn't being discovered. What is he? Is he a disfigured human or a robot? She tiptoes to follow him. They enter a laboratory room; she manages to hide behind a steel cabinet, peeping at the man, the man presses the button on the board, and an electronic machine comes out from underneath the floor where there are four diamond symbol chips to make this machine work wonders.

'Rio! Rio! Cut the damn boy's neck to get out the diamond chip, but please be careful not to destroy them as they are my greatest invention.' Dr. Mark clenches his fist in a clear sign of frustration.

'Alright, everything will be fine, Dr. Mark; stay cool, man,' Rio replies.

After an hour, the drilling of Lucas's neck is successful. Rio takes the tong to pull it out. 'Got it!' He places it into a transparent container. 'I'm going to pass it through the water to clean it,' Rio says.

'No! Whatever you do, please don't wash it. It's an electronic device,' Dr. Mark says whilst gripping Rio by his throat, causing him to choke. Seeing this, Dr. Mark lets him go, and he can breathe as normal again.

Dr. Mark places the chip under the microscope. 'Fine design indeed,' he says, then takes the chip with a tong, presses a button hidden underneath the research table, a few metres from where he is seated, and the floor rumbles as it moves. There are two shutters that slide to the side, giving way for a high technology equipment table to appear. He places one chip on the shape of diamond compartment, and as he does it, places the chip, a bright white and sea green lights shine brightly, blinding Dr. Mark's vision.

'Stop it… Stop it..' Rio, who is fifty metres from Dr Mark, runs at top speed and pulls out the chip from the compartment, stopping the bright light from shining in Dr. Mark's direction. 'Woah!' The bright light of one chip has released a somewhat laser fire that burns Dr. Mark's eyebrow.

Camelia remains silent; she was lucky to find a good hiding place, an empty steel cupboard in the laboratory; she can witness the two men busy activating the digital chips.

She's shocked to have the knowledge of the invention.

Ms. Pediburp enters with another chip, and not knowing what has happened; she places it into the next diamond compartment, which causes a shining light in emerald green to emerge from the chip. She pushes the compartment aside, and the ceiling is shaking like small short waves moving across it, where it ends with a glass covering.

'Good Job Ms. Pediburp,' Dr. Mark says.

'Where is Casendra?' Dr. Mark asks.

Camelia gulps each time he mentions her mum's name.

'She's at the sickbay recuperating, boss,' Ms. Pediburp replies.

'After Rocks and Rio's clumsiness of bringing in a lady instead of my Casendra a few weeks ago, I want both to destroy her at any cost since she's aware of our hideout,' Dr. Mark says sternly.

Camelia grows pale upon hearing this. She freezes temporarily, considering what to do next. It's her that Dr. Mark is mentioning. I need to find a way to escape, or when Rocks or Rio returns to the road or town, I can sneak into their van and be free.

Camelia was about to move away to find an escape route when she sees and hears:

Dr. Mark stares at Camelia's mother's face as she closes her eyes in dreamland after Ms. Pediburp injects a deep sleep serum into the side of her neck. 'She is now mine.'

'Ms. Pediburp, since she's precious to me, please place the detector cuff on both of her legs, and install the spy camera on her dress. Oh God, Ms Pediburp, she is my queen. Why are you dressing her up like a patient? Go and buy her a nice silky dress that a queen would wear, with jewels on her neck, a crown on her beautiful white forehead, and please do something to her hair!' 'We are to prepare her for the connection of diamond symbols power that will be a mass disruption to this small town,' Dr. Mark says.

'Yes, boss,' Ms. Pediburp utters nervously.

'Stop that man, drill his hand, get the chip out now! Unbelievable, Rocks, how could you place our precious chip in your relative's hand? You know very well we'll take it out in a painful way,' Dr. Mark says.

'That was the only solution at the time, boss, he says he will keep it safe.'

'Just an exchange for money,' Dr. Mark snorts.

'He is in a big mess and requires a large sum of money to pay loaners,' Rocks replies.

'Ha! All four chips are gathered as one to become the most powerful technology pressure of the universe,' Dr. Mark says and laughs loudly. He places his diamond shape symbol to combine with the other three as he presses the button to activate the green, bluish and yellow lights. They shine brightly; however, within a few minutes, they are gone. 'What? Where did they go?'

'According to my research and findings, when I was developing this machine, the combination of the four-diamond stone symbols with their electrons, neutrons and human blood, the machine should be working as it's supposed tofour-diamonds I'm flipping the research and findings book, the four diamond symbols will work tremendously with drops of the owner's family's blood. The owner here is you, boss, with Casendra as your beloved, and who else?' Ms. Pediburp says.

'What, the third bloodline of mine? Where do I get the third one?' Dr. Mark says.

'Your child, of course,' says Ms. Pediburp with a grin.

'You are cunning, Ms. Pediburp. So we will see if the young lady is indeed my child. Run along and bring one of her personal items for me to check the DNA,' Dr. Mark says.

'Rocks, you are to find Camelia's hair or saliva for us to undergo DNA,' Ms. Pediburp calls him on the phone.

Camelia swallows her saliva slowly, wondering if the mad scientist is genuinely her father? They had an affair, and I'm the product of it. Her mouth opens widely. No wonder Mum refuses to share her story with me.

While Camelia is lost in her thoughts, suddenly she hears the door bang and finds that Dr. Mark has left the laboratory along with Rio and Ms. Pediburp. 'This is my chance to leave this place.'

Cautiously, she opens the cupboard door without realising Rocks is standing beside her. 'Hey girl, I have been watching you and your whereabouts, so now you know what Dr. Mark is up to. Please hand me some strain of your hair for us to do some testing.' Rocks places his hand out. 'You will be rich in inheritance if you are his daughter,' Rocks continues.

Camelia sees Rocks has caught her, quickly does as she's told, plucks a few strains of her hair and gives them to him.

Rocks smiles after taking her hair so easily. But in her mind, Rocks is being dumb since he chose not to capture nor place Camelia into the sickbay. Due to that, Camelia is free to wander around.

***

'So you got her hair… let's test the DNA, and if it matches with mine, you are to bring her alive. You require my swab, Ms. Pediburp. Bring me the swab apparatus quickly!' Dr. Mark says.

'According to MyHeritage DNA testing results, it matches your blood…she is indeed your family, boss. However, we are yet to confirm the whereabouts of the diamond symbol she inherits or plants,' Ms. Pediburp says.

'Interesting, so she is mine. Let me check the ancient book.' Dr. Mark scampers to the wooden cabinet beside a large portrait of Camelia's mother in his office.

Upon hearing this, Camelia is still shocked by the findings that her father is the mad scientist. She desperately wants to leave this place since she's the bloodline that has the digital diamond chips to complete his madness invasion. She tiptoes out of the laboratory. A few minutes later, she walks for several metres until she reaches the edge of the cave-like place, and is lucky to see a van parked at the entrance. Double joy for her, as the van door click opens when she pulls the knob. She pulls the door, enters, and hides amongst the stuff in the van.

Luck is with her; within a few minutes, she feels the van is moving. 'I'm hungry; let's catch a bite before…' Camelia hears Rio speak to Rocks. The door unlocked when they parked the car. Camelia immediately opens the van back door and quietly jumps out, scrambling to hide near some bushes. She texts Louise, I just escaped. Pick me up.

***

'Where are you?' Louise asks frantically.

'I'm at Burger King, five hundred metres away from Moonsriver Town.'

Louise drives as fast as she can, wearing a mask and sunglasses to prevent Rio and Rocks from recognising her face. Camelia opens the car door and jumps in.

There are so many things happening. Camelia reiterates to Louise what she heard and saw.

'This is outrageous, the man is your birth father, and he is still head over heels in love with your mum.'

'Have you checked the items Gary left for us in the envelope?' Camelia asks.

'Of course not! I was apprehensive about you that I planned to alert Bob if you remained missing for another two hours, making it twenty-four hours as a missing person. Unfortunately, I forgot the existence of the envelope.'

I would be dead if Louise had waited for me that long. Sigh. Camelia thinks to herself.

'Anyways, the most important now you are safe and in one piece. I couldn't think of anything but to save you. I only informed Ben to assist since he is aware that your mum is missing.'

'Let's check out what he has to offer.' Camelia is eager,

with her fingers tearing the opening of the envelope bit by bit.

'It looks like a cigar holder,' Louise says while driving back to Camelia's house. Camelia opens it and pulls out a dark purple velvet pen drive.

After unlocking her house door, they walk hastily toward the room situated at the end of the downstairs hallway and discover the door has been left ajar due to the previous incident.

Camelia and Louise are satisfied the room is vacant and start to insert the pen drive into the Apple monitor. In the video, Camelia's great grandmother Ezra is in black sunglasses with a pillbox hat on her head; cocktail tea party headwear with a black lace veil covering her forehead. With a cigarette in one of her hands while her other hand pushes a paper into a man's hands. He appears to be in his fifties with blonde, greyish hair. 'Look, look at his right hand. Stop, .rewind… what is it?' Camelia tries to widen the image to concentrate on the man's hand; it looks like a bird…an eagle….

Then the camera flips and falls down, and Ezra's voice can be heard saying,' Eliminate him!

'I wonder who Ezra wanted to be killed?' Camelia and Louise glance at each other.

'Let's drive to Ezra's house; the answer should be kept in Ezra or Casendra's room. Anyways what can go wrong? It's your great-grandmother's mansion. You are the next in line.'

Camelia smacks her palms against her forehead then crosses her arms over her chest. She shakes her head side to side.' No! I will not enter the abandoned mansion.' Ever since her great grandmother vanished into thin air, her mother tried to sell this mansion to no avail. Since maintaining the mansion is over her mother's budget, the mansion is now empty and musty.

'You aren't alone, but we won't find any answers if we don't investigate,' Louise says.

'You're right, Louise, let's go; we must find answers to halt this madness,' Camelia says.

***

Camelia scratches her neck. 'The healing process is killing me; it's so itchy and uncomfortable.'

Suddenly the symbol inside it shines.

'Woah! Are you about to explode? Your neck is glowing,' Louise says while parking the car in front of the driveway before entering through the steel gates.

Camelia pulls open the car storage drawer and takes out a small compact mirror to check. 'You're correct, Louise.'

'Get out and help with opening the gate, Cam.'

Camelia does as Louise tells her to, wondering what she's getting herself into by coming here.

As Louise drives further in, she says, 'The house compound looks neat; the grass isn't as tall and messy as expected. I think Ezra's butler must be still living here.

'I'm not sure of the details as Mum refuses to share anything about her past.' Camelia rolls her eyes as she speaks.

'I see a dim light at the top most of the house. Maybe someone is lurking or living.'

They wait for several minutes. Louise breathes in deeply,

unable to imagine what to expect from this visit at the old mansion.

Still, the doors remain shut, and Camelia, who has the key to the mansion, takes out the brass key with a diamond crown holder. Her heart beats faster than usual; she breathes in deeper as she's nervous about whether she's making the right move; her hands are trembling as she inserts the key into the hole and pushes the thick Victorian antique teal wood door in dark brown. It has the trimming of a delicate flower pattern. The hinge makes a sound once the door is open, and from the spot they are standing in, they can see a lovely Chinese wedding antique cupboard in red standing proudly beside the two staircases. Camelia instantly switches on her torch as they step into the house, and they can feel the marble floor is cold as ice with the Persian carpet layout toward the staircase.

Without wasting any time, they climb the wooden antique staircase on the right overlooking the left. Once they reach the third floor, pass room No. 1, and Camelia, without hesitation, opens the second. Louise shines the torch, and they see a messy room with the chairs thrown upside down, teacups with dried lipstick still sitting on the table. 'Let's search for any articles or stuff to prove she had a contract to kill someone. And we must find out who they are.'

Camelia walks straight to the cupboards, opens them, climbs onto a leg stool to bring down a box while Louise checks out the dresser room. Camelia reads out the headlines on a newspaper," Professor Ezra is to sign a twenty-year collaboration contract with Mr. Buttownszki on creating creatures and human invisibility research."

'Maybe this explains Professor Carlos and the furry creatures. I wonder where Jen is,' Louise exclaims.

Suddenly, a heavy thud of boots can be heard amongst the wooden creaks floor.

Hearing this causes, Camelia's eyes open widely. She starts breathing faster, feeling stomach cramps developing. She stands still momentarily, as there is an intruder in this mansion.

'We aren't alone,' Louise whispers in a panicked voice. 'Let me check the other room; I think I saw an opening by the dresser.' She presses the wall; however, no openings appear. But as Camelia stands nearby with her hands on the same wall section, at the same time, the symbol on her neck starts to shine and blinks several times before a sliding door opens. Camelia pushes it wider; Louise shines the torch. They open their mouths to see a lilac coloured liquid in Bunsen in a large laboratory fridge with layers of money and jewellery stacks in the middle of the room. They approach the laboratory fridge.

'I'm taking two of these as a sample– an antidote or a research,' Camelia says. 'Let's go to Mum's room to find information on her lover Chang. He could be the one Ezra wanted to wipe the slate clean?' Camelia says.

They tiptoe, not wanting to bump into any intruder or butler. Camelia's mother's room is kept neatly, the walls are pink, and most of the room setting is like the Covent Garden summer concept with tiny flower petals and wallpaper.

'Where shall we search if we are to hide something?' Louise says. 'Maybe a wardrobe or hiding in a dresser?'

They head for a small dresser room and see it's barren with four pink walls. 'Look, there are drawers around the wall; let's check it out,' Camelia says. They tear out drawers, and flip over her mother's clothes one by one, but no photos or university books are noticeable. As Camelia takes out another drawer, she accidentally drops a brooch on the floor. Upon picking it up, she notices an A4 size box with blue design trimmings, lots of unwanted yellowish papers, and worn out wrappers. Camelia puts those aside and sees two photos of her mother at prom night with two different guys; one is white and looks sturdy and handsome. The photo indicates the guy as Jacob. Another photo shows Camelia's mother holding hands with an Asian guy at the tip of the photo, and it indicates the name Mark with a heart shape. 'Got it! He looks similar to the mad scientist I saw at the cave-like place.'

Camelia's hands are still shifting and flipping the papers in the box. 'The university books, we must take this with us,' Louise says.

Camelia quickly pushes the box into its hiding place. Louise is about to turn the doorknob when they hear footsteps. Both momentarily froze and look at each other. Then, Camelia points her fingers to indicate that they tiptoe toward the door. Luckily for them, although the house is old, its atmosphere and flooring are both silent as a lamb.

Once out from the room, confident there is no one, they climb down the main staircase, two steps away from the ground floor, where they see two dwarf-sized men's shadows near the window on the right side of the entrance door. Camelia and Louise crouch and duck down immediately, step inch by inch downstairs as both are nearer to the ground, and quickly hide beside a Chinese wedding antique cupboard in red, beside the staircase.

'You fool, look where you brought us to Professor Ezra's mansion?' Rio says to Rocks. 'Let's go to the centre fountain area to return to our place. I'm telling you; it's the nearest Rio,' Rocks replies.

Camelia and Louise hear them clearly. They both place their fingers over their mouths to indicate they should remain silent. This must be the intruder's footsteps that we heard; what are their motives? This is suspicious. Have they found the lilac-colored liquid? What will it do? Camelia becomes lost in her thoughts.

They follow Rocks and Rio subtly. Between steps, they hide amongst the covered furniture.

'The fountain should be here in the centre of the hall here, mate,' Rocks says.

Upon reaching a black and greying marble floor with a palm tree in the centre, Rocks takes out a small remote, then disappears into an opening in the floor.

Camelia and Louise head for the centre, where they press the floor and the palm trees to trail their pathways when suddenly the rolling of glass can be heard from the entrance door.

Camelia points her finger to Louise to walk toward the noise. They walk slowly and quietly, and then both duck down, where fortunately for them, there is a bulky sofa that could hide them.

'You're so careless; bring the Bunsen to me!'

'Yes, Sir, I'm sorry,' a man stutters.

'Stop, right now! Who are you, and why are you stealing from my great grandmother's house?' Camelia shouts as she watches them holding several Bunsen tubes containing chemicals in a box.

They run as fast they can, and one of them throws a tube on the floor, which emerges into smoke, blinding Camelia.

Louise chases after them, but the intruders' cars speed away too fast for them to stop them.

Louise catches a glimpse of the car plate before they go and shouts, 'Cam, the registration starts with: 'Butt…'

'Unbelievable, we were so close to catching the intruders. But then we weren't able to see their faces clearly.'

CHAPTER 16

Camelia is relieved to return to her home. 'There are two possibilities on saving your mother, and maybe Dr. Ezra, via the wall in the study or the centre marble floor.'

One thing for sure, there are two different teams of intruders; Rocks & Rio who work with Dr Mark the mad scientist, another…who is 'Butt..' Louise, we need to complete the puzzle of the name Butt… and I have a deep feeling he is Ezra's adversary in the scientific project.'

'And how do we reach it? First, we need to get hold of the two dwarf men,' Camelia says. 'Also, I need to find the ancient leather-looking book; it seems there is some history or a secret gateway.'

'Let's talk in the morning. Too much adventure for today as her head droops on the fluffy white pillow, and she's instantly in dreamland.

After five hours have passed…Camelia suddenly wakes

up from her sleep.

'Argh! What time is it?' Camelia opens one of her eyes to look at the alarm clock and sees it's three in the morning.

'Louise! Get up; a real adventure is coming soon.'

Louise wakes, startled with a wide smile. 'You heard the sound, right? This time I'm accompanying you.'…

They dress up, and the sound dies down, and they both continue sleeping, when within a few minutes, the noise returns, this time much louder. Louise closes her ears with her two hands to get through the banging and drumming sound. She takes a taser baton from her backpack and grips it hard while Camelia prepares herself, holding a chef knife.

This time they're confident and eager to solve the mystery. The door swings open, and they walk out, stop to face the direction of the drumming sound. Camelia points in the downstairs direction while Louise nods. They tiptoe down the staircase swiftly as they'd like to be on time for the opening.

Once their feet reach the ground floor, they quickly grab their sneakers and run as fast as they can toward the noise. As they wriggle their feet into their sneakers, the door starts to shudder; the doorknob tremors and Camelia touches the doorknob; since the tremors are so strong, she can feel them moving into her hands. Then she opens the door, and Louise holds Camelia's light blue jacket to ensure she isn't left behind.

A strong wind like a vacuum pulls them as the door opens widely; the strong wind causes Camelia and Louise's ponytail to be pulled by the current-like forces. 'Ouch! This is painful!'

They release their hands, and their bodies fly into the wall with the ancient leather book on the book racks, and

Louise manages to snatch the ancient book before entering the opening in the wall. 'I hope I'm doing the right thing bringing the book; hopefully, it will help our escape instead of trapping us.'

'It's better to bring it since it looks like it's an opening to somewhere, we could return with it too, you never know.' Camelia is second to this idea.

'Ouch!' They fall onto a pile of sand which covers their faces. 'Yuck!' Louise says.

'Shhh,' Camelia says.

The ceiling appears to be a cave, and Louise blinks twice. Camelia points at the wall where she remembers seeing the two dwarfs and a skinny, fragile lady walking toward it. 'Maybe there are other ways to go through there; let's check out the other side,' Louise says, pointing at the opposite end as they see lights flickering. They walk quietly and cautiously, not wanting to bump into Rio and Rocks. After walking a few metres from the spot, they land near an opening without a door.

'Oh, my love!'

Instantly Camelia and Louise scamper to find a hiding spot, and fortunately, there are bushes and rocks scattered around the so-called caves. So they hide there whilst straining their ears to listen to a man's voice. 'Now my queen, you will be mine forever. You, me, and our child will control the greediness and evil world that wouldn't allow us to be a family earlier,' Dr Mark says as he lays his eyes on Camelia's mother, Casendra's usual rosy cheeks are about to turn icy cold.

Camelia thinks He is destroying her!

Seeing this, she is about to run to her mother's side to save her when Louise pulls her back by her waist and whispers, 'We will be instantaneously caught if you do that!'

Camelia nods at Louise. Her eyes are covered with teardrops. Both can view at their spot, She's dressed beautifully, like a queen with a silk and velvet emerald dress with lace adorned in the centrepiece, and her auburn wavy hair is untied and rests at her waist. Her hand is white as snow, looks smooth like butter. She looks peaceful sleeping. It seems that the mad scientist is maintaining her well. If only she is not cuffed like a prisoner.

'Soon this nightmare will be over, and we will be one happy family,' Dr Mark says, laughing hysterically. Camelia's face turns red, and her hands turn into fists as she's furious seeing her mum suffering, locked up like a prisoner. 'I will never want to live with this mad scientist; I will save my mum and turn him into the cell.'

After Dr. Mark leaves Camelia's mother alone, Camelia and Louise bravely walk toward the room. As they are about to enter, they stare up at the wall where there is a massive portrait of Camelia's mother dressed in a green gown like a queen with a crown adorned with lots of diamonds, and in the background there's a tree with a book which indicates 'Eternal Love.'

They're spellbound with the portrait and the digital equipment set up beside her mother's body. Camelia looks at her mother, seeing her peaceful and beautiful, dressed up as a Victorian queen. 'No wonder this guy is obsessed with my mum. Without her spectacles and light makeup, she's gorgeous.'

A massive pair of rough hands as big as Camelia's face cover her mouth. Camelia startles, kicking his tummy since she's unable to reach his groin; however, her opponent is stronger by twofold, and Camelia's hands are tied with electronic devices, whereas Louise's mouth is stuck with plaster. Camelia feels fearful for her friend and continues kicking her opponent to break free, but her opponent has a sturdy body that isn't affected by her kick.

'Boss, we have someone for you…and there are two this time, Rio says.

'Sorry, Boss, I accidentally pressed the wall gateway, and these two nuisances arrived at our headquarters,' Rocks says, trembling in fear.

'Shush…it isn't a mistake but a benefit. I finally get to meet my daughter. Let me see who is the one that resembles myself and my Casendra,' Dr. Mark says. Camelia glares at him with her eyes bulging; her forehead is frowning with visible layers as lines with her cheek turning red like chillies.

'Rio, does this mean we have a complete set of diamonds to activate our plan?'

'Your mother never contacted me to inform of the birth of my beautiful daughter. What is your name, my dear daughter?' Dr. Mark asks in a gentle tone. First, his hand touches her silky hair, then he holds her chin gently, turning her head left then right, slowly and steadily. He looks dreamy; however, his eyes move from one end to another of Camelia's face as though he's searching for something. This makes her feel a shiver running through her. She hates his touch, as his skin is rough like potato skin.

'My name is Camelia. How do I know you are my real father if you don't know my name?' Camelia asks for reassurance.

'We've tested your DNA, and it matches mine. Here girl, let me show you the data.'

Camelia and Louise blink upon seeing the results of the DNA.

'Come, my dear daughter; we need to take out what is originally my property was stolen by my competitor Dr. Mark Drew. I made all those diamond symbol chips; it was supposed to be a joint project between myself and him. Dr. Drew became greedy and selfish when he found out your mother's Casendra heart is only for me, and her refusal of the contract marriage makes him furious.' He pauses before continuing, 'So one night while I was sleeping at my bunker at the International Research Institute in Moscow, his men caused some commotion until the building was burnt into a burning inferno. While escaping from the fierce fire, a steel rod of the building hit my face and scarred me for life. I'm wearing a half steel mask to cover the unpleasant appearance of my skin; you know how a newspaper is burnt into ashes, that is what my skin looks like.'

'Oh yeah, let me continue telling you about the diamond symbol chip…it contains biometrics, cyber security, and other information systems data embedded in it. It's worth billions of dollars if it were to be sold on a black market. Hence, the only way to protect the diamond chips from falling onto the greedy billionaires is by keeping it safe, without the faintest idea of the hiding place.'

'So the safest place is to insert it into human flesh,' Camelia interrupts.

'Genius, my girl. No wonder you are my daughter.'

'I am sure there are other benefits of the diamond chips other than money?' Camelia asks.

'I will show you tomorrow, enough for today's orientation, ladies. I will show you your room,' Dr Mark says.

'What about my mother? Can't you unfreeze her and let her go? She looks like she's in pain,' Camelia says.

'She is the spark of this mission, and for her internal organs to sustain the power of the chips, she has to remain frozen. I'm sorry, my dear,' Dr. Mark says and appears apologetic.

'How dare you use my mother for your greedy scheme! You are torturing her. Do you even love my mother and me? How did you meet my mother, make her secretly pregnant until she refuses to tell me who you are, your connection with Ezra missing and Dr. Mark Drew?'

'I guess it's normal that you are angry with me due to the recent events. I assure you, I love your mum deeply; as a result, I invented this for her. Since she didn't tell you what happened between us, let me share the whole story from when we met.'

TWENTY FIVE YEARS AGO

I came from Ipoh, Malaysia, with droopy eyes, so people mistook me for being lazy. My face is triangular shaped, my skin is yellow, and my thick hair is short and spiky.

I've always been the lecturer's favourite for all the Science and Information Technology subjects. However, students like to make fun of me, so I feel uncomfortable and sad at the idea of going to university.

After studying, getting an A+ for all the subjects I took, I won several top prizes. Then, one day I met a young lady with auburn curls around her shoulders and a dimple in her smile. She was the granddaughter of the award-winning Biology Professor Ezra Daclan.

She was three years my junior; Casendra, your mother. I fell head over heels seeing such an enchanted beauty walking in the university.

One day, we met at the end of the year university party, where I invited Casendra to the dance floor. At least, until a famous guy named Jacob harassed her in front of other university students. I punched Jacob hard in the face until his nose is broken.

After the dance, your mother spends most of her time with me.

However, your great grandmother Ezra has other plans for Casendra for her benefit ... I continue to be the Head Professor of the University of International Biology and winning the award yearly.

Ezra tries to break up our relationship by her famous influences to assist me in getting a scholarship to further study, invention, and research in such a prestigious International Research of Sciences. However, the only setback I would assume is the location as it's located in Moscow, away from my Casendra. Due to that, I rejected the offer. I worked my way through to be awarded several prestigious awards for my scientific findings and creations, which lends me a scholarship outside town to continue my research and work at the Institute of International Sciences.

A few years later, Casendra contacted me. She sounded down, and we agreed to meet at science awards Night at Hotel La De Cruz. We loved each other, and she came to stay overnight in my room; I think that is the night that we made love. That time, I planned on spiking her drink for preventing her from marrying anyone by mixing her drink with a potion. After drinking, Casendra fainted, and I inserted the liquid to bear me my heir, and the secret coding chip were injected into her armpit.'

As for Ezra, someone who betrayed her must have kidnapped her; I'm not sure what happened to your great grandmother; all I know is she had lots of enemies to achieve prestigious awards. She was too greedy.

'So these are the romance and your scientific career developments events?' Camelia responds.

He nods sullenly.

CHAPTER 17

Scratching his head with his left hand, Dr Mark places his fist on the steel table with a bloodshot wound building from his eye socket. 'Somebody came and stole a majority of my diamond chips!'

Dr. Mark shouts, 'Go and catch the intruder! The intruder has my diamond chips- all three of them, the world will be gone if it falls into the wrong hands. Luckily I am yet to dissect yours.' He is staring at Camelia.'

'Yes, boss,' Rio and Rocks reply nervously at the same time.

Camelia and Louise look at each other, trying to figure out how they can help Dr Mark and free her mother. As they stare at her mother, Camelia exclaims, 'Oh my god! This isn't Mum,' she says, eyes wide with horror.

'What…repeat!' Dr Mark says. 'We're being fooled…this is a mannequin.'

Camelia touches the hair, and it comes off like a wig. The

hands and legs are made of fibreglass.

'Let me check the CCTV. Oh my! The intruder must have burnt all of my CCTV hideout designed as caves.' Dr. Mark frowns, and his cheek grows red in anger.

'What about the spy camera? I'm sure you have installed a spy camera somewhere within my mother, the diamond chips since the items are valuable?' Camelia asks.

'Spot on. You are very bright…Why did I never think of that earlier? Although, I did place a spy detector into your mother's ear hole.'

He wriggles his wristwatch, takes it out, and places it on the panel which is connected to a monitor.

His watch starts to activate a light blue light, blinking, then he presses a button on the panel and several buttons as though there is a password to activate the spy camera. Then a screen appears from the front panel. 'Look, a furry creature? There are two; one is gobbling the diamond chips in his mouth.'

'No! No! He's keeping the chips inside his mouth; look at his mouth; it's not chewing at all,' Camelia exclaims.

'Dr. Mark, the furry creatures aren't your invention?' Louise asks.

'No! No! Of course not; I don't kill people. I only wanted what belongs to me…my love for Casendra, my own family, and to teach Dr. Drew and his billionaire family Mr Buttowski a life lesson to remember.; ifI don't get it, if you don't wish to kill people, than why do you invent digital diamond chips to conquer?'

'Conquering and killing are two different things,

Camelia, my dear. I invented the digital diamond chips to destroy Mr. Buttownszki and his cronies for destroying my good name, invention, my lover, and my handsome face.' Dr. Mark says.

'We're trying to complete the puzzle pieces here. So there is another Dr undergoing an experiment to end or conquer the world or seek revenge?' Camelia says with a sigh.

'Wait! Let me fast forward; where did the furry creatures bring my dear Casendra along with the diamond chips?' Dr. Mark is concentrating the spy camera on the movements of the creature.

'Look! They walked away from one of the walls. There must be an opening for them to go to and fro,' Camelia exclaims.

'Wait, do you know what is this? What does this do?' Camelia takes out the glass tube with a lilac coloured liquid in it.

'Amazing, while I study the results of this liquid and the purpose of this liquid, Camelia, I'd appreciate yours and your friend's return to Dr. Ezra's mansion, the fastest way back to town to catch the intruder who has stolen my chips and Casendra. '

Camelia, being adamant, taps on Louise's shoulder and points in the direction of the wall. 'Dr. Mark, let's try the wall.'

'Alright, guys and ladies, we will try the wall.'

Dr. Mark tosses a radio to Camelia. 'Take this; you may text or send me videos when we are on the move.' He holds Camelia's shoulders. 'Please be careful, as Dr. Drew is murderous.'

Camelia and Louise's hands start to push off the so-called cave wall in the room where her mother disappeared.

'Step aside, ladies,' Rocks says and kicks the wall hard… until the ceiling shudders.

'Stop it. Stop it; you are ruining our headquarters,' Dr. Mark shouts. 'Find another way!

'What about the shortcut to Ezra's mansion? The creatures might be hiding there?' Camelia suggests.

'You are quite right because that is where we found the lilac liquid.' Camelia's eyes twinkle as she knows she's about to solve a mystery.

***

'Dr. Mark, did you kidnap and change Professor Carlos drastically? Please release him this instant!' Camelia shouts.

'What…What are you talking about? Who is Professor Carlos?' Dr. Mark asks.

Camelia shows him a picture from her phone. 'Oh, I think I've heard of him before. He is the best engineer for Data Scientists & Information Technology in town, but why should I kidnap him if I'm known as the global award winning for Information Systems, Chemistry, and biology?'

Camelia and Louise roll their eyes at the same time when Dr. Mark boasts about his success.

'We have no time to lose, quick, let's go!' Rio interrupts.

Within a few minutes, they run to the next secured room with coding to enter. Once they reach the room, Camelia and

Louise exclaim, 'This room is totally different to the last.'

'This is the laboratory with chemicals unlike the previous room, equipped with digital elements,' Rocks replies.

'Come quick ..enter here,' Rio says impatiently. They squeeze into a glass cylinder-like lift, and within a few minutes, they arrive at the centre marble floor of Ezra's mansion. They hide amongst the big vase with green plants located at four corners, just after the centre marble floor opening.

Louise points and says, 'Look! A huge creature's set of footprints is visible heading toward the living room or hallway.'

'Oh my God, there's blood dripping on the floor too, don't tell me it's Mum's,' Camelia whispers nervously.

They tread on the heels of the footprints, and once reaching the living room the footprints seem to be haywire; one goes to the left toward a wall or ceiling, while another veers to the right, toward the hallway and a staircase.

Rio touches the bloodstains on the floor, smells them, and gestures for them to follow. Rocks walks opposite them once Rio signals at him to do so. Camelia is the last in the row, and keeps checking behind her, if any creature is trailing them.

Rumbling sounds can be heard over Camelia's shoulder. The hairs at the back of her neck start to stand up, and her fear is clear on her face. Louise turns to look at Camelia, and she senses something isn't right quickly and changes her position to be last in the row to protect Camelia.

Within a few seconds, two huge, skinless creatures skinless drop from the ceiling, rolling at the centre of their pathway. They get up and screech when they open their mouths. Their eyes are red just like Gummy's, but their growl sounds different from the creature they encountered at Camelia's house. The creature releases its claws and jumps onto Rio, who instantly takes the combat knife from the back of his boots, manoeuvres, twirls on the floor, and extends his muscled arm to stab into the creature's body. Blood drips, however, the creature is still alive and powerful. It screeches as it starts opening its mouth widely, as though screaming in pain, then it starts banging its chest like King Kong.

She doesn't know the appropriate next cause of action, sweat dripping from the side of her hair.

Another creature snatches Camelia, waking her from her fear, 'I need to survive; I'm not a coward.' Suddenly, Camelia manages to place the taser baton against its skinless body; the creature's body tremors and falls flat on the floor; within a few minutes, it starts to get up.

Camelia notices this and immediately pushes the taser baton onto its body twice, and the tremor is too much for it to bear, so it drops flat on the floor with its tongue protruding out.

Rocks walks closer to assist Rio, trying to get his opponent on a spot for him to shoot the creature. He is lucky that he aimed at the right spot, leaving the creature covered with it's blood, and his flesh jumps out from his tummy and lands on the floor.

From a short distance, they hear a harsh voice and more screeching noises. 'The sound must be outside of the entrance, let's go,' Camelia says as she gets up from her crawling position, and Louise starts running at top speed toward the entrance.

Louise opens the door, and they run when they see a tall lady dressed exactly like Ms. Pediburp hastily entering an old green Toyota car and two other skinny creatures. Gunshots fire at Louise from the car's direction and Camelia jumps onto Louise, and they tumble and roll down the entrance steps.

'Are you alright, ladies?' Rocks asks as he reaches the entrance.

'Yup, we're okay,' Camelia and Louise reply simultaneously while getting up and straightening their pants.

Rampaging and clamouring sounds can be heard coming from the main road's direction. This time the sound of creatures growling can be heard louder, and it sounds like there are dozens of them at the main road.

Rio's mobile phone rings.

'Yes, boss.' Rio switches on the speaker and facetime: 'Dr. Mark here, according to my findings of the lilac liquid tube the creatures stole from Ezra's secret laboratory and, the liquid is hazardous, and can multiply a genetic which can turn them into monstrous creatures. The only antidote lies within Casendra and Camelia.' The phone crackles.

'Dr. Mark, you are breaking up,' Louise asks quickly. 'Where in them is the antidote?'

But before he can answer, the phone crackles again, and Dr. Mark is cut off. Camelia curses in frustration and clings to Louise. 'How are we to know the source of the antidote? Also, we need to get hold of my mother. I'm terrified, Louise. Where is she? Can we succeed against a monstrous creature without any science and digital items to protect us? What are we to do?' She starts shaking her head, and her right leg starts shaking like a leaf on a tree branch.

All four of them linger at the mansion's porch discussing their next moves while evaluating the recent events. 'You know what I think? Ms. Pediburp betrayed them; I'm sure it was her who entered the car,' Louise says while Camelia nods in agreement.

'We don't have any evidence to tell them, don't think they will believe us. Let's keep it to ourselves at the moment.' Louise nods at this.

'So now what? How are we to find Dr Drew and his entourage?' Camelia asks Rio.

'Wait…wait. Did you hear that?' Louise asks.

'Silent all!' Rio interrupts.

Suddenly, the mansion shakes, which causes some debris to fall off from the ceiling at the house entrance. 'Woah! What is this? Is the mansion falling apart?' Camelia cries out as some dust and sand drop from the ceiling.

'Run for your life!' Louise pulls Camelia's hand, jumps, and rolls onto the grass as the mansion entrance gives way.

'Phew! That was close,' Camelia says.

***

The land they are standing on feels the tremor of the enormous creature. The sound of people screaming can be heard overlooking the river bank where rich people's boats are parked.

All four of them run toward the overlooking river as the drum, shrieking and loud, comes from the said direction.

Their mouths open widely, while witnessing four furry creatures and a few skinless creatures attacking and smashing the mansion's rooftop at the opposite of the riverbank that they are standing in.

People (neighbours of great grandmother) at the mansion opposite the riverbank run for their lives, some jumping onto the river to hide underneath the boats. Her hands start to shake, and she starts biting her fingernails, thinking of a possible solution.

There are those who panic as the creatures capture them, and the skinny creature squeezes them into an explosion of human flesh and blood, while the furry creatures punch and twist the hearts of women and men, and grotesquely rip into their hearts with their teeth. The more hearts they eat, the bigger and stronger they grow, with their muscles clear.

'Let's not just stand here and do nothing! We'll be the next victims if we don't do something,' Louise says.

Camelia starts shaking her hand badly, starts to walk little steps to and fro; she is thinking whilst feeling nervous.

'What are we to do?' Rocks says.

'You are right Louise, we'd better be safe, ourselves. Let's get into the car and head to my house. It's further than this place. Maybe the creatures are attacking here as Ezra's lilac chemicals are hidden here,' Camelia says confidently.

They enter the Honda Civic that Louise's mother rents.

'Move over, I'm driving,' Rocks says.

Once the car passes the iron gate of Ezra's mansion, chaos can be seen on the road. There are countless bloody bodies with the centre of their chests missing and blood everywhere.

'Pity those innocent people. I need to find the antidote fast to end this madness.' Camelia's stomach starts to churn, seeing so much blood here and there. 'We must hurry to avoid these creatures.'

Louise makes a gagging sound, and her face turns pale. 'I cannot stand the sight and smell anymore.'

Camelia quickly closes the window to prevent the pungent smell of corpses from coming into the car and hugs Louise to give her comfort. 'Let's all wear masks for safety purposes since corpses can bring infectious diseases,' Camelia says.

***

After hours of driving, they finally reach Camelia's house, and here the neighbourhood seems peaceful. The monstrous creatures seem to be surrounded in Ezra's neighbourhood. 'However, it's weird that the creatures don't go into Ezra's compound as though they know their genetic evolution comes from the liquid found in Ezra's hidden laboratory. Or the creatures have been pre-programmed by the creator Dr Drew Buttownszki to cause havoc in that neighbourhood, but for what, and why?'

'There are so many unanswered possibilities,' Camelia says to herself.

'Let me switch on the television so we can watch the news for any strange happenings in town,' she continues.

'All residents are to stay calm and remain locked indoors,' the reporter says.

'Mayor, what and why is this happening?'

'It all happened ten years ago where Dr Mark Drew Buttownszki and Dr Mark Chang,' both photos were shown, 'were appointed to lead the research with the money funded by the Buttownszki Corporation, the research went bizarre and was abandoned when the International Institute Research was burnt down in a wreckage.

The institute's authority was confident the failure research was burnt down along with the fire; however the recent tragedy opposes this. Maybe there is someone behind this that activates the miscalculation of the genetic growth,' the Mayor replies. 'To all the residents within this neighbourhood, be vigilant and stay indoors.'

'Well, can we contact Dr. Mark to find out the next course of action to neutralise genetic growth?' Camelia asks.

***

Reporters surround Buttownszki Corporation, demanding an explanation.

'A mad scientist named Dr. Mark Chang has been making secret visits to Professor Ezra Daclan's mansion and stealing lilac liquid. We believe he has recreated and reactivated the existence of the monstrous creatures. This is him; anyone knows his whereabouts and bring him alive we will give you one million dollars,' Dr. Drew says with a grin.

The television is switched off instantly.

'I don't believe he did that; Dr Mark looks innocent; he is only in love with my mother and wants to start his own family,' Camelia says.

'I concur that Camelia, he is a good-hearted man with a temper,' Rio and Rocks say simultaneously.

'We need to find the evidence that the two men we saw at Ezra's house and stole the liquid is Dr. Drew's man,' Camelia says to Louise.

'How do you suppose we do that?' Louise asks.

'Dr. Mark, answer me please. Dr. Mark…'

'Yes, Camelia, anything?'

'Glad we can connect with you again. We need to know how to activate the antidote.'

'Also, Dr. Drew announced on the television that you are the culprit of the existence of the creatures, so please lay low until we find sufficient evidence.'

'Dr. Drew and his gimmick always want to destroy my reputation! Thanks for the heads up Camelia; I will remain here, and the antidote is to get you and your mother together, along with three diamond symbols to neutralise the haywire genetics. Is Ms. Pediburp with you?' Dr. Mark asks.

'She stabbed us in our backs, boss,' Rio says.

'You mean she is Dr. Drew's spy?' Dr. Mark exclaims.

'Affirmative,' Rio and Rocks say.

***

The screeching and growling return.

'Wake up, Louise!' Camelia says. 'It's spreading toward our neighbourhood; let's get ready to fight or find the antidote. I have the deepest hunch that Mr Drew is the culprit behind the kidnapping of my mother…the last item for the antidote.

Let's pay him a visit.'

They reach the Buttownszki Corporation Headquarters at three in the morning. None of the creatures smell nor see them as they surround the Honda Civic with branches of trees. It was Louise's idea to gum the car's surroundings with tree leaves and branches, so none of the creatures will suspect there are any humans inside.

While on the way to the Headquarters, they have to endure the main road whereby furry creatures and skinny creatures are at large, searching for their prey. The road is stained with fresh flesh and blood with debris from houses as the creatures manage to destroy each and every resident's rooftop.

A head without its body drops on the windscreen, the eyes open wide.

'Argh!' Louise screams.

'Rocks and Camelia will go into the building to find Casendra, I believe she's either at a basement or at the top most floor of a secret laboratory where precious items will be kept,' Rio says.

'Me and Louise will remain in this car to navigate the routes and avoidance to prevent being slaughtered by the greedy Dr Drew.' As he speaks, a black Rolls Royce pulls up in front of the building, and they see Dr Drew in a black leather jacket with dark blue jeans carrying a knapsack as long and huge as the shape of human body. With the assistance of his scientist, the knapsack is placed onto the trolley.

'Let's start the conquer and elimination time,' Dr Drew says.

'The lift opens its door, and a scientist pushes the trolley with the knapsack. One of the scientists says, 'She will die of suffocation, Sir.' They quickly open the thread that was tightening the knapsack to give her some air.

Dr. Drew slaps the scientist across the face. The scientist's cheek turns red. 'Move aside.'

Camelia and Rocks are at the level twelve laboratory area while they're searching for her mother. There are eight laboratories on this floor for them to check, so they move in and out, yet she cannot be found. In one of the laboratories they entered, they nearly blew their identity. A scientist is sleeping at the corner next to the research table in a laboratory. He is sleeping soundly without any noises with his notepad covering his face; therefore, Camelia and Rocks are unaware of his existence. Once Camelia reaches the research table to look for Casendra, she accidentally knocks off the scientist's chair. This jolts him from his sleep and chair. Camelia and Rocks are quick to crouch on the floor. 'Who is there? The scientist asks with his eyes half open. Hearing this, Camelia and Rocks inch step by step to the corner of another table hiding underneath it. The scientist starts walking towards the cabinet, opens it to check. Then he returns to the research table, takes his wristwatch, wears it on his wrist. Yawn. Then he walks towards the exit. He turns his face from the left, centre then to the right, straining his eyes to see if there is any intruders. Satisfy, there is none since the laboratory seems to be still and quiet as an owl at night. He opens the door, switches off the laboratory lights and sped off.

'Roger, they are at the twentieth floor, affirmative there is a lady in the knapsack. I will release the lock to all the doors and floors for your easy movements,' Rio says.

Upon hearing this, Camelia and Rocks left their spot towards the exit of the laboratory.

Rocks pointing at the fire exit. 'The only way they aren't aware of us being here.'

As they reach the fire exit and are about to touch the doorknob, the door springs open, and a scientist in his thirties, his forehead damp with sweat, and breathing deeply, appears. 'I cannot do it; this is not my nature; how do I stop this madness?'

Rocks approaches the scientist by placing his arms against his neck and close to his chest and whispers, 'We are here to help, don't do anything stupid if you want to live.'

'What is your name?'

'I am Dr. Alistair.'

'We overheard you on this mission; we are the good team, we would like to help in stopping this madness mission. So please cooperate.'

He nods.

***

A few minutes later, the scientist named Alistair walks confidently to the twentieth-floor boardroom via the lift. When the lift door opens, Camelia and Rocks reach the fire exit quickly, and Alistair enters with a passcode to the board room. With the promise of cooperation, once Alister opens the door, he lingers near the entrance facing the front of the boardroom. He is buying time for Camelia and Rocks to enter. Then, using his bulky body and medical trolley to ensure no one notices Camelia and Rocks, they sneak up behind Alistair, hiding behind a steel cabinet .in the boardroom.

'Dr Alistair, activate now! The diamond chips are at the main socket. Let's rule the whole world, not only the USA!' Dr. Drew says and laughs.

He takes out the surgery knife, takes out part of her mother's forehead, implants a socket with four diamond shapes, and then places the three diamonds chip onto it.

Camelia bites hard into her blouse sleeves to prevent her from screaming as she sees the suffering her mother has to endure with the hole in her forehead. They are ruining my mother as a revenge for her loving another man, she thinks with tears dripping down her cheek, and wipes it away with her blouse sleeve. She's about to jump out from her hiding place when Rocks pulls her waist and closes her mouth with a cloth. 'Don't you dare do anything stupid! Wait for my instructions,' he whispers into Camelia's ear.

The socket shines brightly toward the computer's monitor, which has readings on it. 'Excellent, Dr Alistair.' Dr Drew walks closer to Camelia's mother, kisses her cheek, and says, 'Goodbye, my love.' Then he takes a lilac liquid from a syringe and injects it into her neck, and within seconds Casendra turns to blink bluish and purple lights all over her hands, face, and chest. It shines so drastically bright that it blinds Dr. Alistair and Dr. Drew and causes both to fall to the floor.

The trolley her mother is lying on breaks into halves. Her body stands immobile, while one of her hands moves, pointing out the glass ceiling, the bluish and purple light flying up in the sky, which causes the sky to drizzle with the liquid that can multiply a genetic which can turn them all into monstrous creatures.

'Soon, all the residents in this town will turn out to be the creatures under my command. They will eat half of the overcrowded world population and reduce the COVID infected people,' Dr Drew says, clenching his jaw.

***

Due to the liquid evaporating and releasing into the sky, those residents that are outside any buildings slowly will turn into furry creatures and skinny monsters.

Rio and Louise are in the van spying and navigating the building, blinking twice as they witness people turning into these creatures when the rain produces a purple and bluish liquid that falls from the sky from the Buttownszki Corporation Headquarters.

Louise is about to pull out the van door when Rio pulls her back by her waist, 'Don't you dare go out there! Do you realize the rain causes people to change to monsters?' Louise's eyes are wide open, amazed and horrified by this statement. She quickly messages Camelia on the change of events happening at her side.

Camelia reads the messages and replies, 'We are doing our best to stop Dr Drew.'

***

'No, you wouldn't have the chance.' Dr Mark suddenly appears from behind the steel table and activates a huge water gun with a Granny Smith coloured liquid. As he's about to pull the trigger to shoot the liquid at Dr Drew, a skinny body shoots Dr Mark in his thigh.

Ms Pediburp- the traitor!

Dr. Drew approaches Dr Mark, seeing he's injured, and as Dr. Mark is about to pull the trigger, Dr Drew manages to take out his gun and shoot at Dr Mark's ribs. Dr Mark flips over and falls, face to the cold floor. 'Dr Mark, finally we meet face to face after such a long time. You look haggard; guess you aren't as well known a scientist as I am.' He laughs. 'I know very well that all the years you kept the diamond digital chips away from me….my money-making intention and disruption of all humans! Today is your elimination day.' Dr Drew smiles with his left hand in a fist and his right hand with a gun, he tries to shoot again since Dr Mark is still breathing and wide awake.

Camelia wriggles and escapes Rocks' grip, crawling underneath the cold floor towards Dr. Drew's direction whilst Rocks distracts him by shooting at the side laboratory cabinet. Dr. Drew faces Rocks, and as he's about to pull a trigger, Camelia tasers him and hits his head with a steel rod that's lying on the floor. Dr Drew's body shakes, then collapses. Then she runs to Dr Mark, grabs the transparent gun, and rolls over to stand beside her mother. She pushes the trigger toward Dr Drew, and he freezes, all ice covering him.

'Gotcha…this is interesting.' Camelia smiles in victory.

'Do I need to be beside my mother to activate the antidotes?' Camelia asks.

Dr Mark, who is losing a lot of blood, as he is about to die, whispers, 'Go quickly, lie down on the next trolley and touch your mother's fingertips, but don't touch her whole body as she is magnetised and has the contaminated liquid inside her. It may spread to you, and there is no cure for that.' Then his eyes lose their lustre, his chest no longer moves, and his head tilts to one side. Camelia instantly shifts his eyelid to close them.

Sweat trickles down Camelia's neck as she's worried.' She touches the tip of her mother's middle finger, and a Granny Smith and bluish light resonate into the sky, and raindrops from the sky, all over the neighbourhood. 'God, please let this work.' Tears linger on her cheek.

***

Rio and Louise, in the van, witness the changes in the residents' appearance and wellbeing. They start to change back to humans and are no longer furry, skinny monstrous creatures.

They smile and hug each other.

Louise calls Camelia, 'You did it…everything is back to normal.'

***

Back at the twentieth-floor laboratory, Camelia is in tears as she discovers her mother's body is lifeless, and she is no longer breathing. Her forehead has a hole in it from the tremendous power circuit that passed through her during the shootout, and the power surge caused all her organs and veins to be burnt. 'Mum, why must you leave me so soon?' She cries and sniffles while holding her mother's hands tightly.

A few minutes later, an ambulance and the FBI arrive. 'Camelia! You are here?' Bob, the FBI agent, walks toward Camelia after seeing a lifeless female from where he is standing and seeing Camelia cheek filled with tears. Once he reaches near the trolley, looking at the state of Casendra's forehead, he gulps. 'This fine lady must be your mother, the one who was being kidnapped, oh my god! I'm sorry that you lost your mother in such a tragic way. I heard you and Rocks are the heroes, saving the whole town. By the way, I have received the report that Professor Edwin and Henry were defrosted once the weird monstrous creatures disappeared,' he tells her.

'That is good news indeed,' Camelia says.

Suddenly, Dr Mark, her mother's body, and Rocks vanish from Camelia's sight. She can see none of them in the room. Feeling bewildered, she touches the steel hospital bed to find her mother's corpse. Then she turns her head left then right and moves her body to check for Rocks, Bob, Dr Mark body, but everything is clear.

Her head is spinning. She is unable to breathe properly as she's feeling something peculiar. 'Louise, where are you?' Camelia shouts. 'Why am I in a hospital bed?' She crumples the bedsheets and pushes the blanket covering her roughly.

Camelia calls out their names and cries in fear as tears roll down her cheek. She walks out from the bed, ducks underneath the trolley and flips the laboratory table cloth to search for them, however in vain. She breathes deeply to maintain her composure as her hands were trembling in fear.

Camelia moves her body back and forth and scratches at

her tousled hair. 'What happened to all of them, they were around a few minutes ago, lots of commotion and blood here and there. It cannot be the cleaners and FBI are too fast to clear the criminal evidence. This doesn't make any sense.'

'Calm down young lady, Dr Mark, your mother, and Louise are in good hands. They are resting,' Dr Drew replies.

***

Once she opens her eyes, she stares up at the white ceiling. She tries to move; however, her hands have been cuffed on the bed, and she feels dazed with the medication they have given her.

'Mum, Louise, Dr Mark…help me. I'm stuck.'

Then a shadow of a man approaches her bedside. The man wearing the white doctor overcoat is smiling at her. Camelia blinks twice, trying to see him more clearly.

'Hi Camelia, I am Dr Drew.' He smiles while refilling the syringe.

Her mouth opens widely upon hearing the name. 'Dr Drew, you are still alive? Who in the world would save you of all people? Camelia shouts loudly.

'Now…now Camelia, you must be having a bad dream. Let me help you.' He smiles with a syringe in his hands.

Seeing this with her half-open eyes. What are those?' Camelia asks drowsily.

'This is a good way to relax your mind,' Dr. Drew replies as he inserts the syringe into Camelia's hand.

'Where am I?' Camelia asks.

'You're in Buttownszki Hospital. You're here to keep your sanity intact after the tragic death of your friends,' Dr. Drew replies with a wide smile.

'No! It cannot be. It's not them. It's you!' Camelia struggles to break free, shaking her head which causes her hair to stand on end.

Dr Drew takes out a taser and shakes Camelia, and the blackness overwhelms her until she falls unconscious.

***

A few minutes pass, Camelia half-awake due to the effect of the medication, walks out from the room, relieved they didn't tie her up, and she's free to roam. She walks out of the room while holding the wall as prevention from falling as she still feels drowsy. However, determined to know Dr. Drew's whereabouts and the plan has caused her to stand, walk and creep around.

Then a few feet she sees Dr Drew's silhouette; she quickly hides behind the medical trolley, not wanting Dr. Drew aware of her tailing him.

Dr Drew walks to the lift to the twentieth floor.

Camelia took another lift to the same floor.

He enters a sophisticated scientific technology laboratory. Camelia arrives just in time to see which room he enters for her to sneak in; her hands are quick to hold on to the hospital door in order not to create any suspicion. She crouches and places her ear next to the wooden surface, hears Dr. Drew and two people's voices talking. Luckily, two chests of medical trolley drawers with six layers are placed beside the door. She hides behind it after opening the door swiftly. From her spot, Camelia can see and hear two scientists named Dr. Alistair and Dr. Ruth are running the clocks to fix Camelia's mother's forehead, where the ignition socket is being placed. While doing this, they had to freeze her body to prevent any damage.

Dr Alistair says,' When can we reactivate the liquid splasher? I should finish connecting it with Camelia's mother as the main point of the socket within an hour or so Dr Drew.'

An hour has passed, Dr Drew comes in, searching impatiently for both scientists so that he can restart his plan.

'One, two, three, four, five, and on!' Dr Drew says.

Together, they activate the three diamonds in Camelia's mother's forehead.

This time, the bluish and purple light flies into the sky through her eyes and shines straight up through the glass ceiling, which causes the sky to drizzle with the liquid.

Seeing this, Camelia closes her mouth to prevent her from shouting, because she knows this would only get her into big trouble.

Dr Alistair switches on a monitor that shows the condition of the town residents; the liquid enters a majority of the town people, which multiplies a genetic which turns them into monstrous creatures. However, some are clever enough to find shelter to avoid getting hit by the strange liquid, so they remain human.

Those who turn into creatures end up eating and killing those alive. It spreads from one town to another; then it travels across the ocean to Tokyo, Seoul, Brisbane, New York, and other places where its government refutes collaboration with Buttownszki Corporation. Lots of citizens lose their lives.

Then Camelia hears a phone call …Dr Drew's voice can be heard speaking.

'All Heads of government, some of your citizens have been eaten by my creatures I have developed and sent them rampaging your country's citizens. Nevertheless, my creatures will not destroy your country if you obey Buttownszki Corporation's business strategy.'

Then from the monitor, Dr. Alistair switched to another channel where there are few top government officials' faces can be seen, appearing worried as the creatures finally arrive at each top government officials' offices and residents as a threat. Seeing this, Dr. Drew takes out a remote from his pocket to stop the control of the creatures from attacking and eating the government officials.

'If you want to save your skin, sign this contract that gives Buttownszki Corporation exclusive rights to all research funds and sales and distributions,' Dr. Drew says.

A few minutes pass, contracts are signed electronically. Dr. Drew smiles as he leaves the room. He's quick before he opens the door; Camelia doesn't realize he caught her by her hand. With his strong strength, he takes out a cuff and cuff her, places a plaster over her mouth.

Since Camelia struggles by kicking him, he immediately sends her to sleep.

***

When Camelia is conscious, she sees herself on the bed in a ward. Television is on as she opens her eyes watching news. 'Reports from the police that all residents are to stay indoors and please avoid any liquid from falling on them.' As the reporter speaks, a screeching sound can be heard in the background.'

Camelia's eyes open widely and she sits upright. 'The creatures are real; I must stop Dr Drew.' She notices a syringe and a piece of paper clip with her health reports are placed on a small side table beside her bed. She quickly grabs it, strengthens the paper clips to make it long and its tip small to be able to be inserted onto the cuff. After a few tries of twitching and shaking, one of her hands is released. Then she tries another and both of her legs. She wriggles both her legs, then moves from the bed and tries to open her ward door, but it's locked. She places the tip of the longish paper clip into the keyhole, shakes and twists it, however, the lock is strong.

She turns her head around to search for any other thicker sharp objects and smiles when she sees a small pair of steel scissors on top of another table, with a cotton and gauze and some ointment. Without any hesitation, she walks fast, grabs it, opens the scissors, uses a side of the scissors, and inserts it into the lock. Since the material of the scissors is stronger than the paper clip, it manages to click open.

Suddenly the door slams open.

Camelia hastily hides behind the door.

She recognises the guy who came in with a cap covering his face.

'It's me, Rio, your dad's friend.' Camelia's eyes twinkle in delight when she sees him. 'I'm here to rescue you and Louise. Meanwhile, let me arm you with the latest invention by your father to catch Dr Mark for good.'

Camelia feels confident now she has a short gun that

has liquid to tranquillise her victim, a so-called epi-pen with chemicals.

They move to Louise's ward; Louise is alert and hugs Camelia with tears falling down her face.

'Louise, I'm giving you a modern electronic taser for protection. We are going to win this fight,' Rio says. Camelia, hearing this feeling excited they, will soon overturned Dr Drew and his cronies.

***

Once they reach the twentieth-floor laboratory, they bump into Dr. Alistair. He runs as fast as possible; however, Rio is faster and grabs him by his collar. He pulls Rio's hand away, trying to escape from the grip.

'I'll let you go if you let us know how to destroy Dr Drew- what is his weaknesses?' Rio says while shaking Dr Alistair hard.

'The ingredients of the lilac liquid plus the antidote finds from the chips. There's a liquid inside those chips, and we need to break it. Dr Drew is extremely allergic to those two liquids, and they will cause him to suffocate.'

Can we trust him? Is he telling us the truth? 'What makes you think he is allergic to those ingredients?' Dr Alistair shows them a scientific report which indicate caution the ingredients will brings fatality to the big boss. Seeing and hearing this, Camelia runs towards the laboratory, and as she opens the door with Rocks behind her, it's in darkness.

Then two strong grips can be felt, one holding her left

arm and another holding her right. She pushes them, her legs kicking out in the air and trying to kick the two masked men. Instead, the two masked men overturn her, cuff her hands and inject her with a tranquilliser.

***

They bring her back to her room.

'Dr. Drew, there is an emergency; your patient Camelia ran away; she went to the twentieth-floor surgery room by herself. Luckily Nurse Samantha saw her walking towards the lift and reported it to us.'

Half drowsy and half-conscious, she snorts at the statement and falls asleep.

***

Camelia holds her head, agony searing in her skull from the medication. Then she hears two voices talking and manages to open one eye. She sees a woman's silhouette. Was it her mother?

'Welcome Dr. Mark and Professor Ezra. Sadly there is no progress thus far on your daughter's mental health. We have had a series of consultations, and all she tells us repeatedly is I'm the bad guy for trying to kill her mother, Casendra and Dr. Mark.' Dr. Drew laughs. 'Her mind seems to be mixed up...swapped with real characters. In her mind, Casendra is her mother, and Ezra is her great-grandmother. Our two assistant nurses, she names Rocks and Rio. Everything seems to be jumbled up in her mind. She is just stubborn… refusing my treatment, she keeps on running away, we have no choice but to inject lithium.' He continues.

'We will try another alternative programme for her.'

'I would suggest you show her your faces, so she knows you are both alive,' Dr. Drew continues.

Upon hearing this, Camelia finally opens two of her eyes wide as she's stunned by the new development. My mother and father are alive… different people. While still resting her head on the pillow, heavy with the reaction of the medication, she continues to see and hear the conversation.

Professor Ezra and Dr. Mark look at each other, blinking bewildered, with this statement.

'Wait. Does this mean my daughter thinks her mother and father are dead?' Camelia hears Professor Ezra ask.

'From what she tells us, that is the way, let me reiterate to you the overall story. She feels she's in it,' Dr. Drew says.

***

After hearing Dr Drew's explanation and reality, Camelia's mind is playing tricks on her. Ezra ponders in deep thoughts.

While Camelia listens to the conversation, she blinks twice and starts sucking her thumb from the right hand, and another starts trembling as her head is confused. Suddenly…

'Camelia, it's me, Ezra, your mother. I'm still alive, my dear.'

Her brows draw together as she is bewildered, the voice….her mum's voice… her mum is alive. But her name isn't Casendra?

'Come and touch my face and hands. 'It's real, isn't it?' Ezra says softly.

Camelia blinks twice. With hands trembling touching Ezra's skin.' Your skin is soft like my mother's. But you aren't my mother; you are an imposter! Professor Ezra is my great-grandmother; she never regards me as her great-granddaughter as she's disgusted by how my mother conceived me!' Camelia shouts.

Suddenly, she kicks Ezra's hand away from her face. Then she gets up on the opposite side of the bed, jumps out, but as she's about to move further, the two male nurses across the room catch her.

'Hold on, let her go, let her express her feelings, and maybe she will feel better,' Ezra says.

Camelia hears Ezra say, then she remains calm and smiles as she looks at Ezra. This lady seems nice, and understanding, just like a mother should be. I feel I can get along with this lady that claims to be my mother, Camelia thinks to herself.

***

Dr Drew comes in as the nurses alert him of Camelia's behaviour toward Professor Ezra.

Upon seeing him, Camelia's eyes nearly pop out, her face turns cherry red, and she manages to snatch a pair of medical scissors from the nurse pocket, jumps on the bed, runs across it, and jumps onto Dr. Drew with the scissors poking into his chest. Fortunately for him, he is wearing the doctor's jacket, which is quite thick, so he only suffers a minor injury.

'Put her in the cell'! Dr. Drew shouts at the nurses.

'Stop it! You are ruining my daughter. All she needs is some love and care to recover from the greatest shock she received after the unfortunate plane crash,' Ezra says while tears roll down her rosy cheeks.

'I am taking half a year's leave to take care of my daughter,' Ezra says.

***

'New treatment begins with her mother Ezra, who will be the main person in handling the care,' Dr Drew says to his assistant nurse. 'Please ensure two nurses remain at her side twenty-four hours a day as her mind is still unstable.'

The new treatment starts with…

'Camelia,' Ezra touches her hand and smiles. 'Two years ago, you, your best friend Jen, and Louise were on a plane returning from Hawaii for a vacation, when unfortunately the plane engine suffered technical problems. You were the sole survivor in the dreadful plane crash. I know it's hard to believe, and I was wrong for not being with you all these years for the treatment. I blame myself for being bogged down with work, withholding the truth on the fate of the plane crash. I wanted the information to remain a secret to protect your emotions; however, I realise one of the cures to your condition is to share and show you the reality.'

'Let me show you the first reality,' Ezra continues.

Camelia reads as written on the tombstone; Louise Armstrong died on the 2nd of August 2021. She places a small bouquet of flower on it, sobbing. Ezra pats her shoulder and points her to the next tombstone. She turns her body facing to the right; she reads, Jennifer Lee died on the 2nd of August 2021.

All of a sudden, her mind recalls the day of the plane crash, and Camelia freezes and her hands clutches her throat.

ABOUT THE AUTHOR

Sherlina Idid studied in Coventry University, United Kingdom and graduated with a BA Hons in International Relations & Politics. She has been working in the human resource management line.

Her interest in traveling has led her to be exposed to other cultures, environments, and sightseeing which eventually sparked her to write her first novel *Mystical Adventure of Ashley Sprinkler (Book Series)*. Eventually her interest in writing expanded into psychological thriller and thriller genre. She can be reached on @sherlinaididauthor on Instagram and as Sherry Ina on facebook.

MORE GRIPPING FANTASIES
AND THRILLERS FROM SHERLINA IDID:

A) Mystical Adventure of Ashley Sprinkler

B) Ashley Sprinkler: Ancient Sacred Twisted Journey
(Out in Qtr 3 2022)

www.ingramcontent.com/pod-product-compliance
Lightning Source LLC
Chambersburg PA
CBHW031253160726
47993CB00001B/140